O FALLEN ANGEL

ALSO BY KATE ZAMBRENO

FICTION
Green Girl

NONFICTION
Heroines

PRAISE FOR
O Fallen Angel

"Like Angela Carter's fairy tales, Kate Zambreno's *O Fallen Angel* deftly exposes the psychic brutality that lies underneath the smooth glassy surface of parable. Set in midwestern America in approximately 2006, Zambreno's characters/ archetypes—a Mommy who names her golden retriever after Scott Peterson's murdered wife Laci, a daughter who signs her suicide note with a smiley face, and a doomed psychotic prophet— are all agents and victims of disinformation, but this doesn't make their pain any less real. In Zambreno's SUV-era America, unhappiness doesn't exist because it can be broken down into treatable diagnostic codes. As she writes, 'Maggie wants to be free but she also wants to be loved and these are polar instincts, which is why she is bipolar, which is a malady of mood.' A brilliant, hilarious debut."

—Chris Kraus

"Kate Zambreno goes for the throat. Or, at least, her language does. Her debut novel, *O Fallen Angel* . . . arrives in the grand spirit of Acker, Artaud, Burroughs, but where these are A and A and B, Kate is Z in full: her own, slick, squealy, and of another light."

—Blake Butler

"Kathy Acker would be proud."

—Karen Finley

"What do you say about an American gospel that beats the shit out of you? I've spent months thinking about it nearly every day, and I've largely given up trying to explain it. It's how you feel at your worst moments; it's less a book than a Molotov cocktail of a story. It will make you think of Acker, sure, but it's a different angel with a different harp. It's something only Kate Zambreno could have done, and it's brave and scared and indispensable."

—Michael Schaub, *Bookslut*

"As usual, the young Zambreno disturbs and delights at once."

—Rachel Hurn, *The Oyster,* "Twenty Novels You Can Read in One Sitting"

"Zambreno turns the Midwest into a bizarro fairytale featuring a psychotic housewife, high-brow literary allusions, and a potent voice that refuses to relent as it links grand themes with whimsical nods to seemingly random aspects of pop culture."

—Lauren Oyler, *Dazed,* "First Books that Don't Suck"

O FALLEN ANGEL

KATE ZAMBRENO

HARPER  PERENNIAL

NEW YORK • LONDON • TORONTO • SYDNEY • NEW DELHI • AUCKLAND

The Malachi section that begins at the bottom of page 28 rewrites a Septimus Smith scene in Virginia Woolf's *Mrs. Dalloway,* as well as borrowing language from it.

HarperCollins books may be purchased for educational, business, or sales promotional use. For information, please e-mail the Special Markets Department at SPsales@harpercollins.com.

P.S.™ is as trademark of HarperCollinsPublishers.

This book was originally published in 2010 by Chiasmus Press.

FIRST HARPER PERENNIAL PAPERBACK PUBLISHED 2017.

Designed by Jamie Kerner

Library of Congress Cataloging-in-Publication Data has been applied for.

ISBN 978-0-06-257268-4 (pbk.)

17 18 19 20 21   LSC   10 9 8 7 6 5 4 3 2 1

TRIPTYCH: AN INTRODUCTION BY LIDIA YUKNAVITCH

I.

Sometimes I fantasize a scene.

The scene is a room. The room is in the Tate Gallery. In the room is a Francis Bacon painting, a triptych to be specific, and a Naugahyde bench for lookers, upon which I sit with Kate Zambreno. We don't say anything. Not to each other, not to the painting, not to the art guard stage left. We just sit there crying together. Almost silently. But for our shoulders occasionally lurching and the grotesque cry-face expressions. Faces and bodies coming undone mirroring Bacon's.

Like twin girl gargoyles. She monsters. Without speech and yet performing selves.

The fantasy makes me deliriously happy, and it always reminds me of the first time I read Kate Zambreno's writing, which also made me deliriously happy. Although I've always had a problem with the word "happy" . . . it's so dumb. So American. I think it would be more accurate to say Kate Zambreno's writing makes me fall into an ecstatic state.

For almost twenty years I ran an independent press. One year, when the top five finalists for our "Undoing the Novel" contest were presented to me anonymously, there were two manuscripts that literally unmade me while I read them. The writing inside the two manuscripts seemed to escape all traditions and forms with such velocity and horrible beauty I couldn't breathe. The stories were about girls and women, daughters and mothers and lovers and half-wives. The stories were about the bodies of actual women living underneath the cover story of American culture, which meant that their bodies were cut and bruised and blushed and mascaraed and beaten and beautified and tortured and adored and killed and desired and silenced and screaming.

I couldn't choose between the two manuscripts, they were each so extraordinary I wanted to run outside and screech like an animal or let all the animals loose or set my hair on fire. It was as if writing had come back to life.

Turns out, both manuscripts were written by Kate Zambreno.

There is no other writer on the planet like Kate Zambreno. She is singular inside language and she rearranges it enough to undo all of signification. Not even Stein, or Woolf, or Acker ever risked as much on the page. My entire adult life, I have waited for novels that make me feel like something radical has happened to me. The occurrence is rare; most novels make me feel like something I've already felt for too long. Sometimes I feel an American shame for what novels have become. I lose hope. When that happens, I return to Kate's novels and reread. Every single time something else explodes on the page as well as in my body. Bomblettes across the territory or art, interrupting our mindless consumer existences, reminding us that we are alive and in relation to language.

II.

This book is a monster triptych. If by monstrous we mean faces and identities caught at the moment of their undoing. The three panels or bodies or voices are Mommy, Maggie, and Malachi. The background is the mundanity of the dysfunctional American family. The foreground is all girl. Gargoyle girl. Girl gone monstrous or mad from the projection of daughter upon her body, hysterical Freudian girl resisting the stupidity of the script placed upon her, acting out lashing out girl clawing her way to an identity.

This is the girl we've made come back to tell us what we've done to her body.

III.

What does the story of a girl and her body literally becoming and unbecoming before our eyes, mean to tell us? Tender grotesque, fragmented whirl, blurry image escaping the frames?

That we must unwrite what has been overwritten in order to resuscitate the girl and the woman buried beneath "girl" and "daughter" and "mother" and "woman."

That new forms and themes on the page are required in order for the social order as we know it to be unmasked.

That a woman writer's life and body cannot ever be torn away from the arrangements and derangements and rearrangements of the stories about her. There is no place between real and imagined. We just posit a place and project it away from ourselves because we are afraid.

That the character of a woman or girl would have to shred the very pages to speak a self. In a true language that risks incomprehensibility, like the madman's or madwoman's—loosened from languages and sifted to the surface like sediments.

Her body the word for it.

Here is the writer risking everything— language, sense, self, her very life—to restory us. I think it is a kind of love.

Lidia Yuknavitch

Every human being is an abyss.
One grows dizzy looking down.

—Georg Büchner's *Woyzeck*

O FALLEN ANGEL

(chorus)

There is a corpse in the center of this story
There is a corpse and it is ignored
No one looks at the corpse
Everyone not-looks at the corpse

There is a gaper's block, it is blocking up traffic
It is in broad daylight, this dead body

There are other corpses that are ignored:
corpses far away in another country
enemy corpses
living corpses
walking corpses
working corpses

But when a mere mortal dies we do not see it
We look we gape but we do not see it
We do not mourn the ordinary

It is nothing like the death of a celebrity
To lose them, these constant images
is to remind ourselves that we will die
We will die, too, yet no one will care

Our deaths will not be televised
Then who will watch it?

MOMMY

She is his Mrs. and he is her Mister the Mommy and Daddy the two of them forever and ever and ever they will never part they will never be apart except when Daddy has to go make the bread and she has to bake it. She stands at the door she stands on her tippytoes to blow him a big kiss. Goodbye Daddy! He brings home the bacon, she fries it up for him bacon and eggs and pancakes and waffles and maple syrup mmm-mmm good what a wholesome meal it is good for you eat up Daddy! All this talk of trimming fat is nonsense Mommy doesn't listen to what she doesn't want to hear. Mommy doesn't know how to change with the tides it is tradition her Mommy made her hubby bacon and eggs and pancakes and waffles and that is what she makes her hubby! She knows how to make her hubby happy! (Hint: it's through his stomach!) And yes her own daddy dropped dead of a heart attack at the age of 50 but one must not think of such things! Yes Mommy is well-trained in the art of good housekeeping. She keeps the house, she stays inside the house because she's only wearing pink slippers! Such dainty feet! She prefers to stay inside the castle her darling hubby has built for her. She is the princess in the castle and she sticks her head out the window when her hubby pulls up in his chariot a fresh tank just off the line she sticks her head out the window she's dizzy she doesn't get much fresh air except when she's puttering around the garden Daddy recognizes her blonde bob just as blonde and sunny as the day he met her when it was down to her waist and he could slip his hand around that waist just a little thing. Of course now she helps Mother Nature it is Honey-Blonde Hi-Lites her tattooed hairdresser tells her he keeps on going lighter and lighter which makes her nervous and nervouser she pats her hair with no small amount of alarm her hairdresser is a boy with tattoos he makes her apprehensive all that black ink on his arms shapes that seem Satanic what does his mother think? It makes her think of her girl Maggie but she doesn't want to think of Maggie does Maggie have tattoos deep dark wells of ink that she's hiding from her mother? And Mommy's lost in thought and Daddy has already come up from the driveway and the security system beeps and the dog is barking and her heart jumps a bit inside she's a nervous person especially lately with everything Maggie's been putting her through and Daddy comes up to her at home at last such a long drive on the highway of life and she puts her little arms around him her short little arms and he pats her on her fanny her large fanny covered in pink sweatpants with the word Juicy on her sweet bottom she loves pink anything pink pink pink and he says Hi Baby and she says Hi Daddy and she's calm and restful because her Prince is here thankgod.

Let us digress a bit to the rear of this housewife: It is quite a fanny. It is the size of one of her new beigey suede seat cushions that she begged hubby to buy even though they're downsizing at the plant (Daddy said yes of course Daddy is always agreeable Always Agree With Your Wife he told his son on his wedding day). Mommy is not in any danger of downsizing. Do these suburban wives' rear ends grow so big from so much time sitting around on their not-so-dainty derrières? This housewife is now as big as a house. Hubby too has a gut on him, that slings over his belt that he keeps on having to loosen and loosen. Too much of Mommy's good cooking! Mommy's had two babies and two grandbabies—Mother Nature is to blame. It's all those buns in the oven that gave her those big buns! And all of the butter for her monumental butt. Butter in everything! Butter and lard! That's the American way! Mommy is a stupendous baker! More than a Good Housekeeper! A Great Housekeeper! But Daddy looks like he has put on the sympathy pounds as well (Daddy is always so sympathetic to Mommy). A moment on their lips forever on their hips! They are both fat. They are not talk-show fat but they are fat nonetheless. But they are happy fat people. When they look at each other they see themselves as two young crazy (yet Catholic) kids in love. Daddy likes the cushion on his baby. More cushion for more pushing! Their darling son Mikey who lives nearby with his darling wife and their darling children bought them one of those newfangled exercise machines one year for Christmas (Mommy would never say X-mas, it's like crossing out Jesus). Every time Mikey comes over he first a) pats the dog a grinning golden retriever "our angel" Mommy calls her b) asks if there's anything to eat because his wifey's not half the cook his Mommy is even though she is half the size and then c) asks if they've been exercising. It is his third thought but it is a thought nonetheless! Mikey is such a thoughtful boy, isn't he? Such an angel. My son is such an angel Mommy says with that ringing in her voice that makes her always sound on the brink of tears to whomever will listen. Mikey asks whether Mommy and Daddy have been exercising really he asks Mommy because Daddy has enough on his plate with the lay-offs at the plant he needs to lay off his feet when he gets home and sink into the beigey sofa and have Mommy scurry around fixing him tasty things to eat, Daddy is a hard-working engineer the hardest working engineer he builds great big SUVs like the ones they all drive. He commutes to the dark bad city every morning he wakes up at 5 am so Mommy can live in her Dreamhouse in the country far far away from all the scary city people alright let's just say it a whisper the scary (black) people they keep on coming closer and closer we keep on moving farther and farther away. Poor Daddy, Daddy's got to rest. But Mommy hasn't been exercising she just simply doesn't have the time she says, what with the dog and Daddy and the housework Mommy doesn't go on the thing. She's scared of it she dusts it once in a while she doesn't know anything about technology that's Daddy's job she doesn't know anything about computers or even how to operate her cell phone and frankly she doesn't care to. If Mommy knew how to do everything then Daddy wouldn't feel as useful and that's not very womanly is it? Daddy shouldn't worry about another lay-off, although it hasn't happened yet thankgod, so it's Mommy's job to make him feel important. What if Mommy went on the great mechanical monstrosity and she tripped and fell because of her short little pudgy legs and fell flat on her face, the red face her hubby holds so dear and kisses so fondly when he walks in the door? And her nose started bleeding! Well, what then? Mommy is capable of imagining all sorts of tragedies—that is what Mommies do best. But really Mommy doesn't like to sweat—it's unpleasant. Mommies don't sweat and Mommies don't poop and Mommies don't fart. They do tinkle. They do go to the little girl's room. They do piddle. (That's what Maggie is doing thinks Mommy piddling her life away! Piddling away her expensive college tuition!) Mikey asks if Mommy has been exercising but he really wants to know if Mommy's taken the dog out for a walk Mikey cares more about the dog than he cares for his poor mother (even though they got the dog after the kids all moved away it was to replace her birdies in her empty nest). Mother have you taken Laci out for a walk? Mommy likes dog names that are human names Laci is the daughter she never had Laci is the name of that poor girl that poor girl whose husband murdered her while she was pregnant with their poor unborn child and everyone thought at first she was missing a poor pregnant lady defenseless and helpless and lost oh lost in the forest and everyone was really a wreck about that, everyone including Mommy. Mommy wept tears and tears for Laci more tears than she has ever wept for her own daughter but Mommy doesn't want to think about that no Mommy doesn't even want to talk about that Maggie has dug herself into her own hole and she will have to dig herself out of it it's called Tough Love! It's a parenting technique. Like guilt and manipulation. But that poor girl she wanted to be a good Mommy and she was killed before she could be a good Mommy and fulfill her destiny like those poor women who get their babies cut out of their bellies not like Maggie no not like Maggie already in her twenties and no real plans to speak of. Maggie who is just going to let her fertility years pass her by yes just pass her by, so selfish, Mommy would have had an suv-full of babies if she could have but her kidneys weren't the best so after Maggie she had to have her tubes tied which is a sin but she went to the priest and he forgave her, Father-Whats-His-Name the Mexican one. He is from El Salvador Hubby corrects her although always mildly gently like soap for newborn babies he is such a gentleman. When she was a little girl she had her whole life mapped out a whole houseful of children! in their pajamas with the footsies for Christmas morning! Mommy and Daddy sleepyeyed but joyous that they could purchase all the presents under the tree! But now Mommy's had all of her insides scooped out like a watermelon and she supposes yes it just wasn't meant to be and God's plan of course who is she to criticize God's plans which work in mysterious ways and she just has to be content to be a Mommy to Laci and to Mikey and to Maggie but Maggie doesn't *let* her love her and of course she's a GrandMommy to the two most precious angels in the world Mikey Junior Junior and Missy. They are all M names M&Ms Molly and Mike that's Mommy and Daddy's names Molly and Mike gave birth to Maggie and Mikey then Mikey married Melissa and then Mikey and Melissa had Mikey Junior Junior and Missy and if there's one more bun in the oven (Mommy has her fingers crossed) it will be another M name maybe Mandy? Or if it's a boy maybe Mark? Or

Matthew? They're both in the Bible it's the only book Daddy has ever read cover to cover. Cover to cover! he says.

Yes Molly is now a Mommy just like she always wanted to be she tells Melissa a story Melissa is her daughter-in-law but she loves her as if she were really her daughter she is so sweet and round and rosy-cheeked and a good Irish-Catholic girl and before she set about the business of having babies she used to be a schoolteacher for retarded children for special children Daddy corrects her gently of course gently Yes you're right honey for special children but not as special as Mikey! Or Mikey Junior Junior! Or of course Missy! This is the story: Ever since Mommy was a little girl she would kneel down and say her prayers and every night she would pray to God for a GOOD CATHOLIC HUSBAND and when she met the man of her dreams her prayer was answered thankgod he was such a GOOD CATHOLIC HUSBAND and she liked Mike, yes she did she LOVED MIKE forever and she was a GOOD WIFE to him and above all else a woman must be GOOD must be polite and cheerful and helpful why couldn't Maggie be more like her cousin Mindy such a good girl yes Daddy even thinks so so nice and helpful and polite and oh she is studying to be a nurse which is what Mommy studied to be before Daddy took her away from the world of work and placed her where she belonged, in her hearth and home, yes Mindy is so lovely Gosh she's like a model Daddy says so gorgeous and well-groomed but she knows her place not like some other M name we can think of but not say. Not all self-involved and self-ish and anything else involving a self which is not very womanly.

MAGGIE

Maggie used to be a good girl and at some point Maggie stopped being a good girl she doesn't know when that was. When she stopped being a good girl.

But deep inside Maggie is still a good girl. She is a good girl who is trying to be bad. She is a good girl who is trying to upchuck the evil she feels inside of her. Her poisoned soul.

That is why Maggie starves herself. That is why Maggie binge-eats and then sticks her finger down her throat and makes gagging noises. Because she is trying to vomit up all the poison, all the poison she has let inside of her, everything bad she has ever let inside of her, and if they knew they wouldn't love her anymore.

It is true if they knew they wouldn't love her anymore. The only way we'll stop loving you is if you're a whore, that's what her father said.

Forgive Me Father For I Have Sinned over and over again.

Mary Magdalene was a prostitute yes Mary Magdalene was a whore yes but Jesus forgave her he forgave her didn't he?

but not her Father no now Maggie is DAMAGED GOODS yes.

her tortured soul

Maggie needs forgiveness.
Maggie needs the great sweaty palm of forgiveness to slap her upside the head.

So Maggie the good Catholic girl has taken a vow of poverty yes a vow of chastity yes she won't let anything inside of her, she gets down on her knees and begs for forgiveness, she gets down on her knees she gets down on her knees

her nose is running her tears are running snotty
down her face he soothes her he smoothes down
her hair then he pushes her down down down a
red halo on his cock

yes
yes
yes

down
down
down

Maggie is on a downward spiral yes Maggie is
on an emotional rollercoaster yes.

Maggie has fallen down the rabbit hole.

Maggie is choking Maggie is drowning in all the
poison she has ever swallowed

so she files her nail she sticks her finger down her
throat Maggie sticks her finger down her throat,
that fingernail chipped with black, the black of
Maggie's soul, here comes the oil up the well—
holy moly it's black gold!

And then Maggie feels numbed and Maggie feels

empty and Maggie forgets Maggie needs to forget Maggie begs forgiveness.

Forgive Me Father For I Have Sinned This Is My Confession

Maggie tries to exorcise everything from her system it comes out through her pores all the demons the demons breathing slowly softly down her neck

Maggie has become her own permanent Lent:
no more sucking
no more breathing
no more sleeping
no more desiring
no more wanting
no more puking
no more drinking
no more going home with strange boys
no more waking up in strange beds
no more walks of shame
no more guilt no more shame
no more no more

Maggie is going to change Maggie is on the straight-and-narrow arrow Maggie is repentant she is Saul she is Paul she is Mary she is Magdalene she is a good Catholic girl.

Yes a good Catholic Midwestern girl she cannot forget her roots they are showing they are light brown through the black.

But then other times Maggie is a very bad girl yes a very bad girl because she doesn't care whether they love her anymore. This is when Maggie is filled with HATE.

This is when Maggie rebels. Maggie has always had an edge on her that Maggie.

It is a razor-edge she files against her nails which she sticks down her throat. It is a razor-edge that she slits her wrists with and out pours the sticky red of her blood and suffering. It pools around her feet.

Maggie is Ophelia.
Maggie is drowning in the whirlpool of her own emotions.

This is why Maggie wears all-black.
She is mourning herself.
She is mourning the void.
She is mourning her world.

Maggie is trying to externalize the demons she

has deep inside. That is why she wears all black and has black nail polish. That, and she enjoys making her mother deeply unhappy.

Maggie why do you have to wear all black it's terribly depressing?

But can't you tell Mother? Can't you tell how dark and brooding I am? I am wearing all black and I am not your sunshine your little sunshine anymore.

bruises for eyes
a bleeding sore for a mouth
a red halo around his cock

The truth however is no matter how dark and demony Maggie tries to be in her heart deep inside she will always be a GOOD MIDWESTERN GIRL.

It is true. She cannot escape it. She cannot escape herself. She cannot escape her mother. She is nice and polite. She is a good girl. She crosses her legs at the ankle. She says I'm Sorry and Excuse Me.

She has difficulties saying No she can't say No to anybody because she wants to be well-liked.

This is why Maggie is so deeply conflicted. She wants to be good and nice and polite and smile at the cashier Maggie you're so pretty when you smile but then she also wants to rebel.

She is a rebel without a cause. She is Natalie Wood in *Splendor in the Grass* and her mother and father keep threatening to put her away, but no this is not the 1950s anymore Mother— Mommy hates when she calls her that—this is not the 1950s anymore you cannot simply put me away.

Maggie cannot be put away. This year Maggie won Most Congenial in her Ward at the Hospital.

You cannot simply put me away in the cupboard she says. I am not one of your ceramic statues to be dusted.

MALACHI

The messages spill out onto the streets. He cannot capture them fast enough. He attempts to pin down these messages, these voices from up above, pin them down on scraps of paper and backs of things. Desperate scribbles on napkins—the messages have a time limit, if he does not write them down NOW NOW NOW they will disappear. Scrawlings on the wall. He mutters them into the air where the words dissipate. He sends them out with great showers of spit to passersby. He speaks in tongues of fire. Blazing Warnings. Fervent Prophesies. He is possessed with this purpose, to communicate. It is a fire burning through him, a spirit. Later he takes out his scraps and spreads them out at the foot of his cave, attempting to stitch together the master narrative, attempting to decipher the higher meaning. The mouth of his cave opens wide, wider, swallowing him up. He will be safe here. A voice, a voice again:

you will be safe here
you will be safe here young man

No no no no! he shuts out the voice. A flash—a small room, the sensation of being strapped down, arms opened out wide, bearing maps of his suffering. There were men in white, yes, men in white, and women too.

He takes out his scraps of paper. Diagrams and designs; little stick women and little stick men with wings on their backs; other stick men brandishing swords; eternal circles around copper pennies, the stern solemn man at the center he is not god no no but is he good?; stars and suns, the source of his creative power; the map of the world, the universe, the heavens. Celestial bodies. Maps of suffering traced out on a small scale of his own body. Over and over again, little spikes of fire, fireballs, fiery stars, comets. A sign? Is this a sign coming from the heavens? The sun that speaks to him. The sun and his daily communication with warmth, light. Perhaps he is meant to burn them. Yes, burn them! He takes out a match, on which is traced one of his stars, symbols. He sets fire onto his paper city. And the Lord rained down fire and brimstone upon the unholy city he chants.

MOMMY

Mommy is a ministering angel, she swoops right in with her wings swoops right in and administers to every cut and bruise and sore feeling. Mommy doesn't always think her daughter-in-law is the BEST wifey for her son her Prince Special Who Can Do No Wrong. Oh these modern women with their modern ways these modern women who go to the movies with their girlfriends once a week (selfish) and then leaves their husbands with a (gasp) frozen dinner (frozen heart). One time Missy had a cold and Melissa didn't take her to the doctor right away. Mommy told her: You have to ask yourself who comes first you or that precious suffering angel! Mommy believes in being a mommy-martyr. Mommy believes in giving one's life for one's children and then when one's children prove unmanageable, then one's grandbabies. It is her vocation. And oh she loves her grandbabies so much! She has a life-size portrait of both of them hanging up next to her fireplace, her blow-up dollies next to the picture of the rose Daddy and Mommy bought at a craft fair. Now that is ART Daddy says not like those squiggly Picassos that look like something the grandbabies did. Gosh look at the gorgeous photograph of the rose with the glistening raindrop on it just like a teardrop. Have I told you the story? Mommy asks Melissa Melissa says Nooo she is a bit bored and Mommy's stories have a way of holding one captive but Melissa was raised nice and polite so she listens. Deep down Melissa isn't that crazy about her mother-in-law not so deep down but Laws are what Melissa was taught and Laws are what she follows. And Family is Tradition and hence very important. Family is the Law of the Land. This was the first rose on the first rosebush after the photographer's mother had just died Mommy pauses for dramatic effect is that a tear we see? a gently placed tear? she is picturing herself dying she is picturing her own funeral there will be lots and lots of pink roses her favorite Yes Mommy loves roses she loves pink pink roses she likes to tend to her garden she likes to pick the flowers herself and fill her home with such love and joy and fragrance yes fragrance Mommy loves to fragrance everything roses because Everything's Coming Up Roses! She uses Wild Rose Shampoo and Wild Rose Laundry Detergent and Wild Rose Room Sanitizer because everything must smell like Roses! Even Fake Roses! Take a sniff of that, honey, isn't that a lovely scent? One must smell the roses after all that is her theme she may not leave the house but her life theme is One Must Smell The Roses. She even had it stenciled onto a sweatshirt. She has all sorts of sayings around the house from cute little things she bought at craft fairs and craft shops. A Woman's Place Is In Her Garden! A Woman's Heart Is In Her Home! I'd Rather Be Crafting! Mommy continues with the story she tells it so slowly Melissa is drifting off And this was the first rose from her rosebush the spring after her death look at the glow behind the photograph it is as if the mother is watching over them Mmm-hmm Melissa says although she is not really listening. Isn't that a lovely story? I do love a story. Mmm-hmm says Melissa she is trying to pay attention she is leaving to unload the brats off on their GrandMommy so she can have some peace and quiet! some ps and qs! and a spa pedicure at the Korean Nail Salon at the local strip mall! but there is always the requisite song-and-dance. Mommy believes deeply in angels and fairies she talks to them all the time they are buzzing around her all like Tinkerbell protecting her yes she has had Guardian Angels especially when she had to be in the hospital to get all of her insides scooped out her mother who lives with them had said Don't you feel like less of a woman now? And she had cried and cried and cried but there was the light at the end of the tunnel, no not that light, the light like twinkling angel dust and she cheered up Charlie, yes, she did she turned that frown upside down and now she is such a saint herself that she lets her Mommy live with her even though her Mommy is not nice at all and is hypercritical. And angels anything with angels angel statues angel fountains that spit out water, Mommy loves loves love and Valentine's Day. Mommy should have stock in Hallmark (but stocks are like gambling). Will you be mine forever Mommy says to her children and Mikey says yes but Maggie has left the nest, she has flown the coop (she was cuckoo so Mommy evicted the bad egg from her nest). Mommy has been stabbed in the heart by Maggie but not in the nice lovey dovey way like Cupid's arrow. Mommy has a cupidity for collecting cupids. In her guest bathroom she has an angel theme (although angels don't shit, angels shit sunbeams and moonlight). There are angel soaps and little angels on her guest towels (which you are not supposed to use) and bronze angels on the sink faucet Mommy had them specially installed. Aren't they all precious? but not as precious as her grandchildren, as Mikey Junior Junior and Missy. Oh they are just the most precious children. Aren't they the most precious children you've ever seen? Look at their fingers yellowed from Cheetos. Mikey Junior Junior is a real BOY isn't he he likes to play with trucks and balls and all the BOY things BOYS like to play with no Mikey that pretty pretty princess doll is for Missy BOYS don't play with those BOYS like to play sports and be rough and tumble but stay off the furniture! GrandMommy has a weak heart, she tells Melissa that she worries about all the sharp and dangerous surfaces inside Melissa's home Mikey Junior Junior almost split his head open the other day all these sharp surfaces Mikey Junior Junior has just started to toddle and he's toddling off everywhere! It gives GrandMommy quite a fright. Why do they always have to go off on their own? Melissa I hope you're watching them at all times! What could happen! Inside GrandMommy's imaginative (dyed) blonde head springs a list eternal of possible catastrophes that could happen inside one's home. And she just watched a TV special on it! Do You Know Where Your Children Are? (Mommy doesn't know where one of her children is but she has already dis-owned her, like when she returned the angel with the broken wing to the Hallmark store and they gave her store credit. But she knows where her grandbabies are at all times thankgod.) Caution is GrandMommy's middle name. Although it's really Marie, like all good Catholic girls. If GrandMommy could she would wrap Mikey Junior Junior and Missy in bubble wrap and keep them safe. Not that MommyMelissa doesn't worry about safety but GrandMommy worries about it more. These modern women have other thoughts on their mind but GrandMommy never has anything on her mind but the children.

MAGGIE

Maggie is broken. Maggie is having a breakdown. Maggie is having a psychic break and it ain't to Bermuda.

Maggie is broken because inside she feels all of these dark messy thoughts it is Chaos and she doesn't know how to express it!

Maggie is broken because Maggie cannot articulate why she feels sad or why she feels angry and that's why therapy does not go too well.

her dark sticky feelings

That is why it is good for her that she only goes to a psychiatrist now, that's the man with the pills. Tell me why you feel that way Maggie but I don't know! I don't know! I just feel lost yes I am a little girl with her redhood lost in the woods and then Grandma turns into a wolf and eats me. That is the nightmare I keep on having.

Maggie keeps on having a nightmare and it is called her life.

Maggie loves the wolf yes Maggie loves the wolf. The hungry boys with their wolfy eyes and wolfy teeth that leave a trail of inconvenient hickeys.

Maggie knows she really wants it. Maggie says no but her eyes say yes.

no
no
no

Maggie says yes but she really means no.

Maggie doesn't say anything which the wolf-boy takes as a good sign and he leaps on her and tears her to pieces.

Maggie gets smashed. She goes out and gets smashed and then she hooks up with her

Prince Charming, she hooks up with her Prince Charming Enough, and he takes her to his place and fingers her while she writhes in pain pretending it's pleasure

because Maggie doesn't want him not to like her. His breath tastes like Old Style like the alcoholic uncle the Vietnam vet who lives on the streets they are not supposed to talk about him. The bad bad wolf jumps her he jumps her bones the corpse of Maggie

and then she leaves in the morning and never sees him again and Maggie pretends she's nonchalant and adult and doesn't care but inside she's hurting hurting and between her legs is throbbing throbbing that's where Maggie keeps her heart.

Maggie fucks boys and pretends it doesn't matter because Maggie is empowered!

and they don't even need to walk her home or buy her breakfast.

Maggie just wants to fuck. Maggie just wants to fuck the pain away.
Maggie is a cavernous hole.
Maggie is a carnival ride.

You can go to town for hours.
Maggie likes it to hurt. Make it hurt.

Sometimes Maggie needs to put a little self-confidence up her nose. It leaves a trail like Hansel & Gretel.

Maggie is poisoned by all the fairytales. Maggie used to dream of Prince Charming, her Savior, her Messiah, and Prince Charming would come and then she would come and they would come together!

But it is not so. Prince Charming is really a wolf in disguise. And then Maggie started to crave the wolves, the hunters, the bad men in the forest.

Maggie likes the not-nice boys who are mean to her.
Maggie likes the not-nice boys who pull her pigtails on the playground.
Maggie likes the not-nice boys who pull down her skirt and push her up against a wall.
Maggie likes the not-nice boys to force her to her knees.
Maggie likes the bullies and Maggie likes the ones who torture her, who deprive her of her sanity, who leave her awake during sleepless

nights wondering what went wrong? what could Maggie have done differently to make him love her?

Maggie is into Xtreme Love like Xtreme Sportz. Maggie needs to wear kneepads because of all the rugburns.

Maggie always lets them get at least to third base which is finger-fucking

usually she lets them get to home plate.

And Sleeping Beauty was slipped a mickey and raped. Or she just let him inside of her because he was pleading and insistent and she wanted him to call her again.

And Sleeping Beauty wanted to be liked and had terribly low self-esteem so when he said that she was the prettiest girl in all the land she gave him a blow job, even though her jaw locks sometimes.

And Sleeping Beauty pretended to be asleep but really she died inside and then she let Prince Charming cum between her tits and on her face and in her hair as he breathed Yeah Bitch Take It.

And Sleeping Beauty didn't make him wear a condom and now she has pelvic inflammatory disease and crotch-itch and genital warts, but oh, the memories.

Don't all little girls have rape fantasies? Maggie is in a dark wood and the wolf comes up to her and he slams her face into a tree. He chops her to pieces, the bad, bad, wolf, because she is a bad, bad, girl.

MOMMY

The happiest time of Mommy and Daddy's lives was when Mikey and Maggie were five and three years old. They were such GOOD children. Such PRECIOUS babies. Such ANGELS. Yes those were some Precious Moments they shared with the children, Mommy and Daddy like to sit and remember, Precious Moments like the cute angel statues Mommy collects in her china cabinet. Children are such angels (their children were, anyway). They had the whitest blond hair like glowing halos they were really angels but then their hair grew brown and darkened. And everything darkened in adolescence, especially Maggie. But when they were their babies, their angels, their dollies. Mommy dressed Maggie in the prettiest dresses and sometimes they would dress alike and Maggie would sit on Mommy's lap and Mommy would comb her hair and teach her how to braid her dolly's hair. And Daddy would play rough-and-tumble games with Mikey, and play sports, and ride bikes, and they were the bestest of friends. Because Mommy and Daddy didn't have adult friends! Their children were their friends! That's what one has children for, anyway, isn't it? Mommy likes children when they're at the age before they start disagreeing with you or knowing more than you do. She hates the idea of FREE WILL. She thinks some children can be selfish, the way they grow up and reject everything spoon-fed to them. She wishes she could freeze Mikey and Maggie when they were five and three, that's the age she would freeze her young tots, she would keep them that age forever, dip them in that freezing vat like strawberries in chocolate fondue! Yum yum. Now Mommy's hungry. Mommy and Daddy get sad thinking about their empty nest. There's no sound Daddy likes more than the laughter of children! It is music to his ears! Sometimes they sit out on their back patio and eat bowls of the Snax Mix bought in bulk at Sam's Club (there are so many different flavors you have to try Chipotle, Bar-B-Q and Honey Mustard) and reminisce about the old days when they heard the sounds of young tots everywhere, or two young tots in particular—their little devil and their little angel, because boys are supposed to be devils and girls are supposed to be angels. Now the tables have turned. Some of the houses in their subdivision have young children and they like to listen to them and Mommy's eyes glisten when she sees their plastic pink bikes with safety wheels (blue for boys) on the front lawn. She wishes her children never took off their safety wheels! Who knew that they would choose to fly fly away from their Mommy and Daddy? Although Mikey didn't fly that far. He lives in a nearby subdivision in a nice house because he's a good boy. Mikey takes care of his parents and isn't that the natural order of things? You have children and then your children grow up and take care of you. They don't leave and move to Chicago and live in a bad neighborhood that they know your Mommy is too frightened to visit. What was wrong with all the in-state schools Mommy would still like to know. Maggie could have settled down here and found a nice boy to marry and Mommy and Daddy would have bought her a new car and helped her with a down payment on a condo before she got married and moved into their new house with empty rooms for the nursery. What was good enough for Mommy and Daddy and Mikey should have been good enough for Maggie. But OH NO. Maggie wanted to move to the BIG CITY far far away from THOSE WHO LOVE HER and now Mikey is practically an only child yes practically an orphan yes it was a big scene and Daddy although Daddy is as benevolent and as kind a man as there ever was Daddy said he did not know who she expected to pay for all of this when Maggie wanted to major in psychology where are the jobs in that? And doesn't Maggie know that Father Always Knows Best? Mommy and Daddy had never heard of such a thing, of such a bad girl obviously rejecting all things good and holy, which is science and tradition. They were always uneasy with her psychology major because psychology after all is a pseudo-science not like engineering! One actually MAKES THINGS in engineering what does a psychologist do Mommy wonders? Except make trouble. Except blame everything on the Mommy, blame everything on the Mommy and Daddy, that's what a psychologist does, and who needs a psychologist when you have Jesus? And parents who love you? God only knows what that Maggie is up to, wanting to drop out of college and wait tables. Mommy could guess but she doesn't want to. Is her little girl on drugs?

Is her little girl having promiscuous sex? Is her little girl in trouble? In the old-fashioned way? God Only Knows. Mommy's attitude towards Maggie is like Bill Clinton's with gays in the military—Don't Ask Don't Tell.

Oh Mommy is getting all a-fluster her red face is growing redder and redder she doesn't want to think about such things. Mommy possesses an amazing ability to drown out the unpleasant things of the world that she doesn't want to think about, especially Maggie. It's quite a talent. The only time she has ever seen Daddy mad is when he gets worked up over their bad girl Maggie. She's a bad seed maybe she's just a bad seed Mommy's mommy says to her, but Mommy won't think about that possibility, she worries sick over Maggie really she does. Mommy thinks of roses but she erases the thorns. Hence the talent Mommy has for pruning in her garden. How could Maggie make Mommy so upset? Doesn't one know that One Should Respect One's Elders? It's in the Bible! Honor Thy Mommy and Daddy! Do Not Take the Name of the Lord in Vain! Which Maggie certainly has to Mommy and Daddy's faces! Some very unpleasant words Mommy doesn't like to hear! Which Mommy doesn't care to repeat! No Mommy doesn't care to repeat!

MALACHI

He spreads out his leaves on the concrete. They scatter to the wind. Did he write these frantic missives? He does not remember. Revelations on napkins. Messages from the dead. From up high. Perhaps they have been translated by God. Not touched by his hands.

a great fireball will erupt from the sky

one cannot reason anymore with the President

one life for the life of
thousands

lies lies lies
airplanes

warlords
profit
false idols
prophet

He has been sent here, he has been sent here by
God for what? He is the messenger angel. He
has come down to warn the people, warn them
of what? He reads his missives over again. One
life for the life of thousands. Who is that one
life? A great fireball from the sky. Airplanes.
Malachi has a vision of airplanes exploding,
falling from the sky at a great height. Is this
how God will rain down his great vengeance
for wars of lies and false idols? A rain of fire.
A rain of airplanes. A flash: paper airplanes.
A young boy's hands. That's right! Malachi
remembers, suddenly, excitedly. I have a sun!
A son! That's right! That's right! Malachi
remembers. He has a son somewhere. But
where? And what does this have to do with
his mission? He has a son, he named him after
himself, he crafted him in his own image.
Malachi #1 and Malachi #2. He writes down
on the back of the classifieds, found near the
dumpster (he is in his cave):

He will inherit the earth.

He must find his sun. Yes, his son. MALACHI. The messenger angel. The prophet that will not be believed. He must venture forth in this murderous world of sharp sounds and find his descendent. He has scattered this seed. And then, another flash: they have murdered him! Yes, yes, they have murdered his son! His own flesh and blood! They have poisoned his thoughts against him! He hurries out in the street. He must go find him! He must recover him from enemy forces! He must explain! Explain how he is not really sick! No, he has been gifted, gifted with these voices and vision! These REVELATIONS sent to him from up high! He has been instructed to give it all up and follow these messages! The sun blinds him. He shields himself from this source of life, light. He listens as the sun speaks to him. Soldier, you must retreat. Yes, retreat. It is not safe now. It is not time. You must be on your mission. You must sacrifice your son, yes sacrifice, for the Greater Good.

A flash: an army of toy soldiers. He is small, fuzzy, indistinct. A man looms over him. His father, his daddy?

Line them up
Line them up

Malachi retreats back to his cave. Some of his scraps are lost forever. Lost forever. Torn away flitting to the wind. Two messages stuck together in a small puddle sharing a home with dampened cigarette butts and the shine of a gum wrapper. A shine. A sign.

one life for the life of
thousands
&
a great fireball will erupt from the sky

One is part of an ad for a 1-800 number. A busty black woman looks at him. She is Large & Lovely. She wants to know if he is looking for a good time. The other is a book of matches from the gas station off the highway. A Book of Matches. He must match them together. A Book of Fire. Some sort of sign. He tucks the scraps into the pocket of his fatigues and heads off towards the gas station.

MAGGIE

Maggie likes the bad boys, yes, Maggie likes the bad men, but why Maggie when you have such a nice father?

Maggie likes the wounded soldiers. She likes the fallen angels. She likes the devil types, like her blond Lucifer.

Maggie likes the Dark + Handsome, Dark + Mysterious, Dark + Brooding types she likes the Marlon Brando types the James Dean types the rebels without a cause and she is the nice Natalie Wood who wants to go on the wrong side of the tracks.

Once Maggie laid down on the tracks but the

train didn't come and she got up again. That was Attempt #1.

Maggie-the-Cat has 9 lives she wishes they would hurry it up already and be done with.

If Maggie was a cat she would be a black cat and you better not cross her path.

Maggie is very deep she is a deep well she is a black hole you cannot look down her although you can look down her blouse whenever you'd like, if you tell her she's pretty.

Maggie is afraid of falling, but Maggies loves to fall in love.

Maggie is always falling in love, with unworthy boys who destroy her.

Maggie is currently quite sad because she's torn up over a boy. He's torn her to pieces.

She keeps on waiting for him to rescue her and he never comes.

She likes the bad boys the ones that are bad for her. Maggie is SELF-DESTRUCTIVE. She has the love instinct and the death instinct and they are in an eternal cage match inside her head.

This latest boy is playing with Maggie's head.
Maggie is boy-crazy.
This boy has made her crazy.

He is the cook at the restaurant where she waits tables, he is blond and devilish and has thin sinewy biceps and reads Nietzsche. He drinks Scotch out of the bottle which he chases with milk because of his ulcer which is because he feels so deeply, he is deeply tormented

he chases his Scotch with milk and Maggie chases him.

He is the silent tortured type, like Marlon Brando with the stringy blond hair and overcoat in *Last Tango in Paris*. Maggie likes the silent brooding type.

She is so desperately in love with this boy, she is so honestly, truthfully, agonizingly head over her heels in love. He doesn't say much about the subject. Maggie consults a daisy as oracle. He loves her he loves her not but secretly she hopes he loves her!

He doesn't want to get involved, but he lets her give him a blow job over by the meat cooler.

He can't get too close to people, but he lets her come over (just this once!) and he fucks her without a condom (Maggie doesn't know how to say no) and then refuses to hold her.

She beats at the wall of his hollow frame—Say something, say something dammit!

Her blond devil cook has a terrible temper, he is like the abusive father she always dreamed of having. He once even put his fist through a wall! Over some girl he was in love with! But not over Maggie because he doesn't think of her that way.

Oh Maggie dreams that someday her Marlon Brando will grow to love her in that way that he will tell her what to wear and who to see and put his fist through walls in jealous rages over her.

Maggie wants nothing more than to be slapped around a little, she wants to be punished, she wants to be punished for her bad, bad, soul. This the boy obliges in bed, and that's why she can't forget him, they concoct fairytales where he has driven her far out into the woods and has tied her up and gagged her and beaten her senseless and Maggie shivers because she can only imagine the depths of such love.

But Marlon Brando has now run away with Maggie's best friend and Maggie is crazed with grief. She writes him little notes but she receives no answer. She leaves desperate cries for help on his voicemail but he does not return her calls.

He has left her with nothing but his memory and that inconvenient case of genital warts.

Maggie just wants to die! She just wants to be put out of her misery! She must get a job at a new restaurant, one of those chains where she has to wear a tie and mention two appetizers by name upon greeting, because she cannot bear seeing the boy anymore, although sometimes she walks by his apartment building hoping to see him still.

And with Time + Distance, perhaps this great love will dissipate and she will forget, she will sink into a hopeful amnesia, but did Romeo forget Juliet? No he did not.

And anyway the first cut is the deepest.

MOMMY

Mommy goes kind of deaf when the news is on and anything unpleasant occurs like wars or hungry children in Haiti or global warming, Mommy tsk-tsks and changes the channel or fixes herself a snack in the microwave. She watches her stories that she follows religiously or she watches the talk shows. She relaxes into the banalities of daytime television it is a calm sea she welcomes familiar faces she loves her talk shows she loves chatting and gabbing but she doesn't like to actually talk about anything real. She loves Oprah even though Oprah is black she is a very articulate black woman yes a very gentle black woman yes there's nothing racist about Mommy how could there be something racist about Mommy when she watches *Oprah*? And reads books from the book club? Although Mommy won't read Toni Morrison because Mommy doesn't read depressing books or watch depressing movies especially not ones about child abuse and slavery. Mommy likes books about shopping or romance or mysteries or better yet romantic shopping mysteries. Mommy likes books with stiletto heels on the pink cover. Anything pink. Pink, pink, pink. Think pink! Don't think at all! Mommy would live in a pink castle if she could. Sometimes Melissa and Mommy talk about what was on *Oprah*. Melissa and Mommy watch TV separately when they're going about their morning routine although Melissa is still an active mommy she is still on active duty so she possesses more purpose in the morning and Mommy misses that feeling of purpose.

The whole family likes to watch TV—they gather around it, it is their altar. Usually when the grandbabies are over Mommy pops in a video because she gets so tired! It's best for the grandbabies to sit still or they might hurt themselves! Especially Missy she is three and needs to learn to sit like a lady! Which is on your ass watching the television! It's best to practice the assumed position of apathy and defeat! The family especially like the dating shows, the shows when a man courts a bevy of blonde barbie dolls with the hope that one beauty will become his wife his life and they will live happily ever after. And the others that aren't good enough to be The One are still good enough to make out in hot tubs with, as they all look good in bikinis. Every night the family watches the man who is a rich and handsome bachelor, just like in the romance novels, they wait breathless with anticipation over who will receive his roses to stay in the castle and continue catfighting over him. They all love that show Mikey and Melissa and Mommy and Daddy. They trash the girls they don't like she's not that pretty, she's too jiggly, she's not a natural blonde, she's dumb (a girl must not be too smart no that's a smarty-pants but one must not be too dumb well not too too dumb). On TV one is supposed to be perfect and if one is not than that is a cardinal sin, it's different than real-life expectations. Mommy likes the girl who is going to stay a virgin until marriage but she doesn't like the slutty ones. The worst crime on these shows is if a woman is easy although she can't be too difficult either that's high-maintenance. Even with her sweet sweet mouth Mommy will say That Woman's a Whore and think nothing of it not thinking of her best pal Jesus and how he let Mary Magdalene tickle his feet with her hair and her whore-tears. That woman's too easy Mommy will say and Melissa and Mikey and Daddy will concur (although secretly Mikey and Daddy like to see the big boobies and the itsy-bitsy bikinis and they store it all in their head later for a good whack-off in the shower, well Mikey at least, not Daddy Daddy has been defeated by a lifetime of domesticity). It is okay for a woman to be easy as in simple but not okay for a woman to be easy as in loose. After she's married then she can wear the loose-fitting sweatpants. Then her birth canal can open right up and out will slip Baby #1, 2, 3 at least two or what's the use of getting married anyway? Nice girls don't open their legs, even if it's in the hot tub and in front of TV cameras, not without a ring on their finger. Mommy likes the brunette girls the best, better than the blonde ones because they are more modest but she doesn't like the ones who seem: Jewish, black, or brown if it's not a tan. Not for my boy, she will think. She imagines all these women as brides competing for her son, who has already been defeated in marriage, by a woman Mommy didn't pick out herself. Not that she's saying anything about his choice! And Mikey was a catch, yes he was, he was a catch. Her Mikey is such a wonderful father such a good father such a steady boy Mommy says. Is Melissa a wonderful mother? This is not something Mommy goes on and on about, this is not really something Mommy can say. She is a good mother, yes, but is she a great mother? A GRAND mother? Times were different in my day, that's what she will say. Mommy is always diplomatic and never gossipy. Oh never! Melissa you just seem so tired honey I can see it in your eyes let me take the children from you I mean for you. Mommy's eyes grow greedy at the thought of taking the children. She has such a burning love for her children. She wants to stand guardian over them 4-ever. She wishes she could take the children 4-ever and ever sometimes she struggles against the impulse to snatch the children away in the middle of the night to kidnap the children. Oh isn't it so sad about that little Jon Benet Mommy will say to Melissa I cried tears real tears for that precious little princess what a beauty how could anybody do anything to harm such an innocent precious body, children are angels they are they are angels sent to this earth! Why do they always have to molest the pretty blonde girl-children?

Mommy worries herself sick. Mommy worries, worries, worries. Mommy twists herself up worrying like the dishrag she is holding at the present moment! Mommy worries at the thought of hands molesting her darling granddaughter Missy, Missy is pretty enough to be molested so we need to make sure she is watched at all times and I know Melissa you have your hands full with Mikey Junior Junior so Mommy will volunteer for the cause! Mikey Junior Junior can stay with his parents, after all a boy needs his father. Oh Missy is such an angel she is so much like Maggie was when she was younger oh Mommy misses those days Maggie the prodigal daughter just like in the Bible and if Maggie came back she would welcome her with open arms. What if Maggie comes home any day knocked up! Mommy worries! And refusing to get married! And what a terrible fate for a beautiful white baby to be born out of wedlock! Mommy wishes she had put a lock on Maggie's door so Maggie could never have escaped! Or a Chastity Belt! And only Mommy had the key! Jesus is the key to your happiness Mommy tells Maggie but Maggie doesn't listen Maggie says terrible things like she doesn't believe in God how can you not believe in God Mommy gasps! Mommy covers her ears! Such blasphemy! They are simple God-fearing people how could Maggie not fear God? Or at least her Daddy? If Maggie had a baby she would refuse to baptize it Mommy is sure

Mommy thinks of this often she worries over the fate of her unborn grandchild although she doesn't worry over the fate of her actual born child and then what if the baby died and then its soul would be trapped in limbo that shows what a hateful girl Maggie really is to allow such a thing to happen to her unborn child. Mommy believes firmly in the afterlife that's when her and her hubby will be reunited forever and ever and they will sit on clouds and watch always good TV how can there be no afterlife with no afterlife there's no afterwife? So Mommy has made a pact with herself that if Maggie did have a baby Mommy would snatch it and baptize it under her sink the one with the angel faucets Mommy would dribble water over the baby's little misshapen head such a soft skull so impressionable and Mommy would be the GodMommy! Which is better than having a HeathenMommy! Mommy will save her soul! Of all the possible horrible terrible things to happen to a young girl one must be well-protected! By skinnydipping into the waters of Christ! All the ways one can be molested! One must use protection, spiritual protection of course (not that Mommy has ever talked to Maggie about the other kind, don't ask don't tell).

MAGGIE

Sometimes Maggie feels such terrible mute pain she has such a desire to scream but no sound comes out. Or she yearns to cut off her tongue so she cannot scream ever again.

This is when Maggie takes a razorblade, the edge she has on her, and slices into her skin, just a little, just to feel the burn, just to feel pain. But Maggie only makes surface wounds. It's mostly for show. She chisels on her wrist a little and then shows the boy next day. See how much you've hurt me? See how much I suffer?

Maggie wishes the world could see how much she suffers. But maybe one day yes very soon she will seal the deal, she will open the floodgates and out will pour the red river of her suffering, and it won't be Aunt Flo coming to town. And then Marlon Brando will come to her funeral and is that a tear we see? and then he will know how much Maggie really loved him, she loved him so much she gave up her life for him.

Sometimes Maggie just wants to feel something. Othertimes Maggie just wants to feel nothing.

These are Maggie's public displays of hurt. She has been hurt, yes, she has been hurt, Maggie is a public wound. Maggie has gone to bed with strangers Maggie has gone to bed with strangers for affection Maggie has gone to bed with strangers for money just that one time it was for cab fare. Maggie has done all types of things because Maggie is deeply fucked up.

Yes Maggie feels things so intensely there must be something wrong with her!

Maggie is terribly lonely now without the boy or the best friend and she lays awake at night alone and wonders whether she even exists at all.

It is like her mind is occupied territory which

Marlon Brando has colonized. He is all she thinks about breathes about reads about talks about eats about pukes out her pretty little brains about (and who is there to hold her hair?).

O a more tortured soul than Maggie there never was.

Maggie writes in her Dear Dear Diary about herself vs. the world, but mostly she just writes about how she misses Marlon Brando and all of his predecessors (and likely successors).

The best way to get inside Maggie's pants (heart) is to be withholding. Catholic girls crave denial. Remember that one night when we were doing Ecstasy and we were so in love? she writes Marlon Brando. Maggie likes boys with a taste for sadism and Maker's Mark on their tongue.

Maggie has an addictive personality
Maggie is Addicted to LOVE
The pink pill which says "LUV" on it. The pink pill that says "SEX" on it.
Maggie confuses sex with luv
Be Mine 4-Ever

MOMMY

Mommy believes fullheartedly in the sacred institution of marriage. She believes strongly in family values and the importance of the nuclear family. It's the American way the nuclear family the nuclear bomb the white picket fence. Mommy thinks fences are important because they keep out the undesirables like illegal aliens. God appointed Man and Woman to be together. Daddy thinks this too he gets quite impassioned talking about the subject It's Adam and Eve not Adam and Steve! It's in the Book! The Big Book! The only Book that matters! Sodom and Gomorrah! The men they wanted to rape the angels! That's what those homosexuals are they want to rape the angels by that we mean our poor defenseless children! Mommy and Daddy believe in relations but not that type of relations! One must guard oneself against the threat of homosexuality at all costs, it is staining the pure white fabric of society! Mommy's brother is an interior decorator in Miami and he is a homosexual and it makes Mommy uncomfortable to think about. Mommy doesn't talk to the brother she has evicted him from her nest although he is allowed to come home for Mommy's Famous Thanksgiving with Mommy's Famous Turkey Dressing (hint: raisins!) but only if he comes alone and acts normal enough not all flagrant or flaming like the Burning Bush that talks to Moses like fairies talk to Mommy but not that type of fairy. Mommy doesn't need this evil to infect her children like AIDS. Children are so pure and good children are very susceptible at that age and they need to be taught the rights and wrongs that's what parents are for.

Mikey Junior is very alert to the dangers of Mikey Junior Junior turning into a homosexual, by that he means not becoming a star athlete. Mikey Junior is the golf pro at the local country club. Mikey Junior works with very rich people at the local country club, but he wishes that he could have been a major golf star and gone on all of the tours and tournaments, and at that he failed. Mikey Junior, who is a failed athlete, has made it his life purpose to make sure Mikey Junior Junior doesn't fail, and more so, that he doesn't turn out to be a faggot. Because nothing's worse than being a faggot! The threat of being a faggot, or a sissy, or light in the loafers, as Mommy puts it, delicately, with a little giggle (referring to the choir director at the church) is lurking around every corner and so Mikey Junior must protect his son his own blood from that! Mikey Junior gave his life so that his son might live! When Mikey Junior Junior turned one years old his father began feeding him protein shakes! Because Mikey Junior Junior is going to be big and strong and tough and not cry like a stupid sissy! Boys are rough-and-tumble! Boys Don't Cry! Boys are Big and Tough and Strong! Boys don't play with dolls maybe they play with Action Figures but certainly not dolls! Boys don't play with girl toys, like paints and books! Boys play with boy toys! They play Cops and Robbers and Cowboys and Indians and all the fun games Mikey Junior played when he was little, tying up Maggie to the tree until she got rug burns and locking her in the closet when they played prison! When Mikey Junior Junior even looks at one of his sister's girly dolls his father throws the ball at him!

Fetch! Sit! He's training his dog well! Be a Man he tells him! Be a Man! Don't Be a Failure! Hit the ball through the hoop! Hit the ball with the bat! Don't throw like a girl! Don't hit like a girl! Don't be a girl! The process of indoctrination is fervent, and must begin at birth so you make sure you don't get a softball. However much Mikey Junior Junior tries and tries he will never be as good as Mikey Junior wants him to be. Oh how selfless Mikey Junior is! He is already working double-time with private lessons to save up to send Mikey Junior Junior someday to expensive summer sports camps, the ones he really wanted to go to but his selfish parents wouldn't send him to maybe they could have if they had just scrapped and saved and sacrificed some more! Mikey Junior wants his son to grow up just like him but just Better! Faster! Stronger! With hotter chicks after him! He picked Melissa because she was good mommy material, that pleasant smile, those hips, like a hostess at your local Cracker Barrel! She's the girl next door, which is good for Mikey Junior because he doesn't like to leave the neighborhood! And that was easy enough to go next door to get her! Mommy played Cupid in this whole whirlwind romance she bought Mikey Junior tickets to the Ice Capades to take Melissa. Good to show her that you're cultured (they were engaged nine months, why take it slow? they knew what they wanted 3 babies before 30, a house in the suburbs). Melissa wanted babies so badly she had their names picked out already! And boy Melissa proved to be one Fertile Myrtle they only had to try once for Missy. On the honeymoon night Mikey Junior was plastered out of his mind but his shooters shot straight (as befitting a golfer). But he shot off the mark because he wanted a boy, a man about the house, one to carry on his name, so they had to try again even while Melissa was still recovering from the c-section! Yes Melissa was a good choice, a good mother for his children even though Melissa doesn't look like those girls in their bikinis on TV! And good for her that Melissa breastfed Mommy says. Mommy is always asking questions of the most intimate nature but that's because she cares! Women who don't breastfeed are terrible mothers! Good thing Melissa isn't a terrible mother! These parents want to literally reproduce their childhood! Except taking all the bad stuff out, like when Mikey Junior lost the state championship. Mikey Junior can't wait until Mikey Junior Junior starts playing sports at a competitive level and he can go to all of his T-Ball and Little League games and his basketball and soccer games, oh boy, he can play lots of sports, play the field, but at some point he has to stop fooling around and get serious, in order to get a college scholarship (to Mikey and Mikey Junior's alma mater of course) and then he has to be the BEST GOLFER THAT EVER WAS! If Mikey Junior Junior doesn't pick golf Mikey Junior will be awfully disappointed, but as long as he's some sort of professional athlete he will be pleased. But Mikey Junior has already put a golf club in Mikey Junior Junior's hand and he seemed to like it! He even took a swing! And hopefully Mikey Junior Junior will one day be one of the very rich people at the country club (it is such a prestigious club women cannot join and it's whites only!) instead of having to teach the pruney women and deeply tanned men how to swing! That's Mikey Junior's dream for Mikey Junior Junior! To be a have, and not a have-not. Mikey Junior wants Mikey Junior Junior to have everything, everything that Mikey Junior has ever wanted but nothing more! It's the American Dream!

So Mikey Junior is never home, no never home it's really just Melissa and the kids, which is the way she wanted it, she really just wanted a sperm donor and a provider she's wanted to have babies since she was little! Isn't that what every little girl dreams of, a Barbie Dream House and Ken, even if Ken is never home and is usually grumpy? And anyway one learns that life doesn't always end up like a beautiful fairytale she doesn't have a prince but at least she has her castle! Or a nice home in a good area! If Mikey Junior gets to have the parenting responsibilities of molding Mikey Junior Junior, then he lets Melissa have Missy, who has already started out on gymnastics lessons and ballet lessons and at-home piano lessons taught by Melissa who was taught by her Mommy (mostly popular songs from musicals like *Cats*). Although she'll always be Daddy's Little Girl! Mommy even got Missy a pink T-shirt that says that! Daddy's Little Girl! Maggie used to be Daddy's Little Girl didn't she she would sit on Daddy's lap while he was watching baseball remember Daddy remember our darling, our precious? Oh and she is depriving Daddy of the greatest joy in life, which would have been paying for her wedding, and her gorgeous white wedding gown, and Daddy could have walked his daughter down the aisle and given her away! But they've already given her away which means they have lost hope! She is hopeless! Melissa and Mikey Junior's wedding was a very nice affair, yes very nice, although Mommy didn't get to have as pivotal role as she would have liked, because Melissa already has a Mommy, thankyouverymuch, a Mommy who is a bit classier than Mommy and attends fundraisers at the art museum which makes Mommy very nervous. But oh it was a beautiful wedding wasn't it yes the bridesmaids dressed in pink she had six bridesmaids no Maggie wasn't a bridesmaid but her cousin Mindy was! Oh she was gorgeous! Mommy was quite nervous at Mikey Junior's wedding oh yes she was happy so happy ecstatic maybe too happy which is why Mommy had to take some of her Valium before the proceedings she was just all a-flutter and a-fluster no she is not very good at social situations where she feels everyone (Melissa's family) is judging her! Mommy's eyes cloud with tears when she thinks about those people, the second set of grandparents, if you ask Mommy they are the inferior set, although Melissa's daddy was so happy when Mikey Junior Junior was born! So excited he bought him a hunting cap! He can't wait to take him hunting and shoot deer no not Bambi of course not Bambi stupid deer that overpopulate anyway and morning doves those are nice targets. But Mommy doesn't want to think about the other Grandparents (GrandMommy #2 and GrandDaddy #2) nor how they spent Easter over there this year when

Mommy was so excited about the chocolate Easter bunnies and oh the Easter egg hunt just like when the kids were little, Baby do you remember yes Honey I remember! Yes Daddy used to dream of walking his daughter down the aisle but now he has a back-up dream, which is to take the grandbabies to Disney World! Which is such a magical place! And of course like every proper little girl Missy wants nothing more than to be a princess! You are a princess already Mommy tells her! Isn't she a princess isn't she precious yes precious she is the pride and joy of our lives Mommy says. Girls are sugar and spice and everything nice, yes they are. Such a sweet girl and look how she plays with her dolls she is so maternal Mommy tells Melissa, who agrees. Look at how she plays house (which Mommy shows her how to do) daddies sit at the front of the table and mommies serve the daddies! And oh oh how Missy loves her GrandMommy! Missy is all light and sunshine and angel kisses! Her little angel! Sometimes when Missy is sleeping Mommy just wants to devour her, she just wants to eat her up, num num num, like the witch in Hansel & Gretel, she loves Mikey Junior Junior too but Mikey Junior Junior is loved specially by his GrandDaddy, who throws him up on his shoulders so he can see how high he can rise in the big great world (but not high enough to exceed your elders) because that's how things should be, it's the natural order of things and Mommy is very strict about the natural order of things! Mommy is the disciple of the natural order of things the God-given American-made order of things.

MAGGIE

Yes Maggie is a troubled girl. You can tell she is troubled because she stares with a faraway look on her face when she is supposed to be taking your order. She is quite thoughtful, she is quite reflective, her face is like a reflective surface.

Maggie has just read Sartre and so she is seeing the world with new eyes. What is the reason for existence? Maggie doesn't know. Maggie feels nausea too but perhaps it's just love pangs or hunger pangs.

Maggie feels different from the rest she feels strange she feels estranged but she doesn't know how to express it.

Maggie doesn't want to be different. Maggie *is* different.

Maggie doesn't want to be part of the flock, if Maggie was a sheep she'd dye herself black!

Maggie doesn't know how to express this difference she feels from the world, this sense of being apart and watching, watching by the salad station when she should be filling up dressings! Maggie is not very articulate about what she is thinking, but what she is feeling is very intense.

Maggie feels and then acts and then thinks, which apparently is the wrong order of things.

Maggie wants to be FREE but she also wants to be LOVED and these are polar instincts, which is why she is bipolar, which is a malady of mood.

Maggie has recently been diagnosed as bipolar (her new nameplate reads Hi! I'm bipolar! Can I take your order?) which explains all the bad self-destructive decisions Maggie has made in her life, such as dropping out of school and getting involved with Marlon Brando.

Maggie is like the rotten apple—it was good, and

then it became rotten. Maggie has been spoiled maybe that's why she became a bad apple. Maggie is like the poisoned apple, and she choked on it, and died, but now she is being brought back to life because of modern medicine! They brought her out of the DARKNESS and into the LIGHT.

Sometimes Maggie wants to black out and forget the world, and then someone sees the girl slumped in her own puke and calls 911.

Maggie saw the LIGHT and wanted to go towards it but they resurrected her! They brought her back! She's alive! She's alive!

Now Maggie mostly feels like a zombie.

Maggie is chock-full with enough pills to choke a horse! Currently Maggie is prescribed a cocktail of pills for her bipolar disorder. Maggie accepts her diagnosis, she wears it proudly. Maggie used to rage against the machine but now she accepts it with open arms and lets it feed her pills.

Maggie used to do lots of bad drugs but now she doesn't have to because she has her drugs prescribed for her! Uppers in the morning downers to go nighty-night.

Maggie's pills are so pretty. The dark mood stabilizer like a little lentil that stains her fingers red. The anti-depressant, the sleeping pills, the anti-anxiety. She doesn't like the Lithium it makes her feel terribly bloated.

Maggie works hard to be a working member of society. There is woefully no cure for what she has but there's a lifetime prescription! That her health insurance probably won't cover! If she ever does have her own health insurance (Daddy has kicked her off his health insurance. One must stand on one's own two feet! Daddy says).

Too bad Maggie has no real marketable skills. Maggie will be forced to work with the masses, who don't realize that really she's a princess in disguise, waiting tables and bringing you more ketchup, I'll be right with you Sir.

Maggie doesn't sit well with labels. Her doctor has met other Maggies before but Maggie doesn't think so, Maggie is unique! Maggie is different! and not just in that snowflake way.

Maggie, snap out of it! Maggie come back to Earth we need you to take these nice people's orders! Maggie are you high? Maggie are you on drugs? Maggie is on lots and lots of drugs but they are all legal! But before that Maggie did illegal drugs, which are the bad kinds!

Maggie never learned to Just Say No! Maggie only learned to say yes, yes, yes, please, thankyou verymuch.

Where were the warning signs? Maybe when Maggie started hanging with the Bad Crowd.

Maggie is a cautionary tale, a cautionary tale of caving into peer pressure. Maggie is an after-school special.

Maggie got hooked, yes she did, on drugs. Maggie hooked, yes, she did, once or twice. Oh, and does sleeping with a boy to get: drugs, dinner, a taxi ride home, attention, a bag of groceries, a job, help with moving, count as selling one's body?

Maggie has sold her body to the highest bidder. Maggie has sold her soul to the highest bidder. Maggie has sold her soul to the blond Lucifer who has chewed it up and spit it out.

Now Maggie has a better drug pusher, she has a drug pusher with a cushy office, a drug pusher who really cares about her and calls her every day and listens, really listens to her complaints, every physical ailment, no, not her feelings, Maggie isn't feeling much of anything nowadays except numb and bloated.

Maggie started having panic attacks where she couldn't speak. Large crowds coming at her while she forced her way through, the brutal door buzzer that made her jumpy.

She went to the doctor. There there he said. There there he patted her hand. You're a bit nervous, aren't you? There there. There there.

Maggie turned herself into the Authorities. Begging for Bellevue and Bedlam and Bible Study. Instead she got a photocopied hand-out on panic attacks and a list of shrinks that carried her father's insurance.

How would you do it? They asked. They wanted to know if Maggie had a PLAN.

That's all everyone wants to know: What are you PLANNING on doing? What is your PLAN? (Your five-year PLAN your lifetime PLAN.) Maggie doesn't have a PLAN for killing herself. Maggie prefers to kill herself slowly. So they didn't listen to her. So now Maggie has a PLAN, and she's storing up all the little pills that she doesn't take.

(chorus)

They are erased from the family album
these corpses that are ignored

homeless on the streets

They become lepers to the good Christian families
but didn't their Jesus lick the leper's sores?

and when it happens
and when it happens

Mommy's baby overdosed
someone else blew his brains out

They always cross themselves and say, as if like
a prayer

It was nobody's fault
It was nobody's fault

For the men crucified next to Christ were, after
all, common criminals

This allows them to be able to sleep at night to
not be haunted
          haunted by

the torment of dark thieves

MOMMY

Mommy sometimes pictures Maggie's funeral like she pictures her own funeral. In each fantasy Mommy will be the star although Maggie will be the corpse the corpse in the center of the room. Mommy hates the word 'corpse' it gives her shivers. It will all be very sad but most importantly everyone in the room will know that IT IS NOT THE PARENTS' FAULT that Mommy and Daddy did all they could but their daughter was manic-depressive-bipolar-schizophrenic or something, Mommy couldn't really pay attention to all the unpleasantness in the doctor's office. Mommy will be very relieved when Maggie is gone she just wants to be relieved of this GUILT Mommy feels that is so paralyzing. She was perfect when they had her she wants to tell the world she was perfect and not flawed no hairline chips or cracks she wasn't cracked she was a good girl she was wholesome she was whole it was only when she went out into the bad world and their evil influences that Maggie cracked and fell and broke like Humpty Dumpty a bad egg and Mommy will dress Maggie finally Maggie will let Mommy dress her Maggie won't have a choice Mommy doesn't believe in choice Mommy will dress her in that nice flowery dress she bought her last Christmas that Maggie turned her nose up at but she won't have a choice now! No she won't have a choice now and finally Maggie will be her girl yes her girl and she will visit her grave every Sunday and place pink roses yes pink roses at her grave and maybe plant a begonia bush and her tombstone will read Maggie Our Precious Angel . . .

Mommy is a near-hysteric and Maggie sends Mommy right over that edge. Oh Mommy Dearest. Mommy needs to take a chill pill, which is called a Valium, which Mommy gets in the generic from the doctor for special purposes such as weddings and funerals, and then for general purposes such as life. A few glasses of wine too would do the trick but Mommy doesn't drink, she doesn't like to be vulnerable in front of other people, she doesn't like that feeling of letting herself go. What's the use with all that freedom Mommy thinks. Mommy let the parade of Women's Lib pass her right by, she was on her knees cleaning the floor at the time. Mommy cleans all the time cleanliness before godliness! that's what Mommy says. Everything in her home is: white, beige and pink. The colors of Mommy's big maternal breast. Mommy scrubs, scrubs, on her knees. Actually since Mommy's gotten a bit older and heavier it's harder to go down on her knees so she hires a Mexican woman to come in once a week and clean. But no one is supposed to know about that! Yes a Mexican woman her name is—what is her name? Maria Mommy thinks— the poor woman is an illegal and doesn't speak any English! Mommy can't imagine someone being so stupid as to not know any English. It's a disgrace, really, a disgrace, to be so unAmerican. Mommy certainly doesn't know any other languages but she certainly knows English. Why would she need to learn any other languages? Mommy can visit Europe when she goes to Epcot Center. Her favorite country is France—except in her France, the waiters are clean and nice and she gets to eat crepes! Mercy buckets! Anyway Maria just does the big cleaning jobs Mommy can't handle anymore, but Mommy stands over her and directs her. Mommy is not-so-secretly fearful that Maria will steal from her, because that is what the help is known to do, especially the Mexicans, one must watch them at all times. Mommy still does the day-to-day cleaning. Mommy makes sure everything in her castle is straightened just-so. But then Daddy comes home or the grandbabies come over and Mommy makes a meal and it's all a mess again! One has to start then from the beginning. It makes Mommy very tired not that she's one to complain! But lately Mommy and Daddy have been ordering a lot of take-out in Styrofoam containers, buffalo wings and hamburgers and steak and french fries. They throw the Styrofoam containers away because they do not recycle because global warming doesn't exist! The polar bears are fine! Mommy and Daddy saw them at the zoo when they took the grandbabies! Global warming is a fiction dreamed up by the Communists! Who are trying to take Daddy's job away! Mikey Junior thinks so too he says to Mommy the weather seems fine out here it doesn't seem to change I don't really believe in this global warming stuff. Mommy agrees with her sweet boy. Big strong SUVs are as American as big strong men and weak frail mommies. So to recycle would be to admit that Daddy makes evil gas-guzzling monsters, which of course Mommy and Daddy would never do. The land they prefer to live in (besides Disney World) is Oblivion. It is a nice land of Valium cocktails and cable TV!

MALACHI

They pretend not to see him. He stands at the mouth of the highway, and they roar past him in their metal cages. These metal cages that keep out the outside world, the unpleasant reality. They do not see him. They choose not to see him. His inconvenient prophesies. They are willfully blind. They do not care about being saved. They do not want to KNOW. How they are hurrying towards the End, the End that is near, in their metal cages, their oil-guzzling monster trunks, their battle tanks, that devour up the lives of innocents. How, how, can they not see what is there? How can they ignore what is in front of their faces?

The sun, the sun it speaks to him.

He holds his face towards it. These people yes they are all prisoners prisoners of their thoughts their minds like small cages. They do not want to hear the truth. They are deaf and dumb to the truth. Small towns small minds middle class middle of the world middle meddled muddled

He holds up signs of elegant simplicity. Today's sign was instructed to him from on high.

THE MEN THAT LEAD YOU ARE EVIL
DO NOT GO LIKE FLOCKS OF SHEEP

He holds this sign up to the battery chasing each other down the blazing concrete. Like dogs chasing their tails. A barren landscape.

THE MEN THAT LEAD YOU ARE EVIL
DO NOT GO LIKE FLOCKS OF SHEEP

It is a simple sign but they do not look him in the eyes, no, the eyes that know, the mouth that speaks TRUTH.

THE MEN THAT LEAD YOU ARE EVIL
DO NOT GO LIKE FLOCKS OF SHEEP

They can be lead like sheep by the Butcher Men,

the Butcher Men that have slaughtered leagues of innocents. For what? For the black gold that powers the monsters he watches chase each other, a dizzying blur? RUSH HOUR. Everything is a rush, everything is fast, fast, fast. They slow down for no man. Dark speed-monsters that are the signing bonus of a pact with the red-faced Devil. He of horns. He in disguise. He allowed to live among mortals. He allowed to conduct evil, to murder, to thieve, and to stay on this earth in opulent grandeur. There is no Judgment Day for the Devil while on Earth.

It is hot today; yes; it is Hades. The end, the end, will have the sun setting on the ground, setting the city ablaze with furious fire. And only he, only he will be saved. He and his family. He and his mirror, his Malachi. Because he believed; because he spread the message. And his face was as it were the sun, and his feet as pillars of fire.

He wanders over to the Quick-E-Stop. He is hungry. He is thirsty. He wishes for a cup of water. A bit of change. Citizens stagger out from the doors, holding foot-long candy bars like swords, Big Slurps and satiated expressions. Citizens fed a steady diet of lies, lies, lies.

He swallows up the air, the trees, the sun. They will nourish him.

He walks past the fill-up station. Words flash before his eyes—a message. He stops and studies it.

UNITED STATES OF AMERICA—LOVE IT OR LEAVE IT!!!!

GOD BLESS AMERICA!!!

STOP BY OUR CONVENIENCE STORE TO STOCK UP ON SNACKS!!

WOULD YOU LIKE A RECEIPT?

PRESS YES OR NO
THANK YOU FOR YOUR VISIT!!!

MAGGIE

When did our good girl Maggie begin to spoil? Did her parents leave her out in the sun for too long? Let's go back to the beginning. The Genesis of Bad Maggie. The Void, the Darkness. Maggie was involved with team sports, which is a good way to join and be a member of society. Maggie was very involved in synchronized swimming, like a little Esther Williams, just a little fish she was. Maggie was on the B honor roll every semester!

When did Maggie start to drop out, and hook up? Maggie got involved with a bad crowd in the big bad city. Maggie wanted to go live in the big city, she wanted to get away, she wanted to be on her own, she wanted to be FREE. They were burn-outs, they were burned out by society. They wore black and didn't play by the rules. Maggie thought they were the key to being FREE.

Maggie is a life-experience masochist.

Maggie looks for saviors in wild-haired Jesuses.

When did Maggie crack, the bad egg, the Humpty-Dumpty who had a big fall? All the king's horses and all the king's men, they all teamed up on Maggie and Maggie was too wasted to notice. Maggie just sort of blacked out. Maggie has frequent dizzy spells now—it's a side effect of her medicines. It's the side effect of living.

Now Maggie stays home and watches TV. She keeps her own clock by the TV. It dictates her daily rhythms. It tells her when to take her medicines. When Maggie can't sleep Maggie watches the 6 o'clock, then the 8 o'clock, then the 10 o'clock morning news. They all tell the same story over and over. Maggie hates the cheesy banter between anchor Barbie and anchor Ken.

Maggie used to be lots of fun but Maggie has become so serious lately. All Maggie wants to discuss is her current mental state. When Maggie was in college Maggie studied psychology because Maggie is fascinated by herself.

Maggie is having a BREAKDOWN. Her apartment is a mess her mother would never go inside. Maggie lives off the clothes on her floor. Her dishes have been piled up moldy for weeks.

Maggie feels that she is falling, into what she doesn't know . . . Maggie is suffering from benign vertigo.

Maggie is uncomfortable in her own skin, she just wants to peel it off peel it off.

The years line up like dull tombstones for Maggie.

Maggie has no patience for the practicalities of life. Maggie chain-smokes and watches sitcoms. She especially likes sitcoms where there's a love triangle. Maggie was never good at geometry, but Maggie understands love triangles. She lights a cigarette and thinks blankly about Marlon Brando, her Ex, and her Ex-Best Friend.

EX Marks Maggie's Spot.

Was Marlon Brando the cause of Maggie's breakdown? The seeds were planted long ago. There were Warning Signs but everyone chose to ignore them, mostly because Maggie still had a smile on her face. Maggie is a liar. Maggie wears the lie on her face. Can I take your order? Would you be interested in the spinach artichoke dip, or perhaps the BBQ wings to start with?

Maggie is a bipolar werewolf. Maggie sleeps for 17 hours a day. Maggie is always sleeping now. She is zonked out from all the drugs. She doesn't like the way they make her feel.

Maggie is a rebel without a cause. Good, polite, Catholic Midwestern Maggie who has so passively acquiesced to everything decides to go off her meds. She wants to remember what it's like to feel. She wants to feel her demons breathing, slowly, down her neck. The demons that make her do things. The demons that make her self-destruct.

Maggie self-destructs! On the 6 o'clock news.

Maggie is a RAGE of hormones. Maggie is a MESS of body chemicals. Maggie is a hormonal milkshake.

Maggie is depressed. Maggie LIKES to be depressed. Maggie writes in her dear, dear, diary (tear drops stain the ink):

Perhaps love is a delusion and we all hide ourselves with half-lies and fiction.

Maggie writes to fill in her anonymous sketched outline. Maggie is a blank slate.

Maggie is beginning to realize the life truth that no one else knows who anyone else truly is inside.

Maggie's inner life is radically different than people's outward perception of Maggie, which makes Maggie desperately unhappy.

Maggie knows from psychology that the happiest are those with the most illusions. That is Sigmund Freud.

This is why Maggie is not happy—she has lost her illusions.

Maggie is a lost girl. Maggie is drifting in a sea of anonymity and anomie. Maggie likes having sex with anonymous strangers. Blank faces.

The medicine makes Maggie put on the pounds. She is beginning to look like her mother. Maggie wears an overcoat to hide her body, hide herself, shield her face from stares.

Erase, erase.

Maggy is fat but not happy-fat.
Maggie wants to fall apart.

Everything's been so bleak and dumb lately for Maggie. Maggie's life is thin and hollow like listening to her voice on the answering machine.

Erase, erase.

Maggie wants to wake up. Maggie wants to fall asleep.

Maggie yearns. Maggie yearns to be different.

Sometimes Maggie hates herself. That's why Maggie wants to kill herself. Maggie wants to end everything.

Erase, erase.

Other times she wants to kill Marlon Brando, or her mother. But she cannot kill her mother, so she wants to kill herself.

Maggie still yearns for Marlon Brando. Maggie won't let something go until she has murdered it.

She loses herself and she wants to find herself in a personal savior and she touches the next-in-line, a pimply kid with father issues—Tag You're It!

Sometimes Maggie thinks she's so close to drinking iced tea and smoking menthols like the crazies who come in for half-off pizza days which is Mondays. Maggie is serving pizzas now because serving pizzas is easier although the metal tray gets hot. The crazies are from the nearby Section 8 housing. They make messy sculptures with the Sweet'N Low packets. Maggie tries not to make eye contact with them.

Maggie's neck is paralyzed she had to call into work she can't move. She has carried far too many heavy trays or perhaps she is in love with her father. It's hard to say. But Maggie will probably quit the pizza job, which is her third waitressing job in the past year.

Maggie doesn't want to wait anymore. She wants to get it all done with.

Maggie is good at getting fired. Maggie has burned out.

Maggie is a flame-out. Maggie walks through fire.

The other job Maggie walked out of, simply walked out of, saying, no, not for me. Maggie cannot act in bad faith. The job with the tie and the corporate slogans and the dropping two appetizers by name upon greeting was not Maggie's authentic self. Maggie knows that EXISTENCE precedes ESSENCE. Maggie is alive she knows that but why?

More than anything Maggie is afraid of going on autopilot and dying inside.

Which is why Maggie went off her meds. Which is why Maggie went back on her meds.

Which is why Maggie doesn't do her dishes or housework. If Maggie pushes herself to the end is there some sort of award at the finish line Maggie wonders? "She always did the dishes and held a steady job." What is there to live for? Maggie wonders. What's Maggie's purpose?

When Maggie is alone she is afraid she doesn't exist so she watches TV. She watches the boob tube and turns into a boob herself. She doesn't clean or do the dishes or file her taxes.

Maggie is currently low-functioning.

The drugs make Maggie crampy. They give her the chills and the night sweats and the shits.

How lonely it is for Maggie to be so adapted to disguising her SECRET SELF. Maggie is a throbbing, public wound. But she keeps it all inside. Maggie wants to SCREAM but she can't and she wants to BREAK THINGS but she's paralyzed and she wants to CHANGE but it's complicated.

Maggie is scared to live because she is scared to die because she does not believe in God.

Above all else Maggie wants to kill her mother and father, but especially her mother, which is a crime, the highest crime, which makes Maggie feel even guiltier. Maggie lives in a Greek tragedy inside her messed-up head.

Mother Dear Who Bred Our Wolves' Raw Fury

But Maggie cannot kill others so Maggie murders herself. Which she does by sleeping all the time and not leaving the house.

Maggie's living her life, no one's living it for her!

Maggie has to be cut from her mother's apron strings (umbilical cord).

Maggie wants no strings attached.

Maggie wants to fuck'n'run.

Maggie stores up her medicines like a squirrel. Maggie is carving out an escape route.

Maggie has a plan.

Maggie wants to wreak revenge upon the world, by that she means Marlon Brando and her parents. She'll show them, she'll show all of them. She'll go CRAZY and then she won't have to be nice anymore. Maggie is MAD. By that we mean Maggie is ANGRY.

And the world will go on living and soon forget

any pale breath Maggie breathed on it. Any timid step she made (baby steps!).

Why are you so tortured Maggie? Maggie is tortured still by childbirth she is still recovering she never asked to be brought into this world a bright pink screaming question mark.

With a great big slap she was brought into this world.

Maggie has been mourning herself since she was born. Maggie was born in a repressive regime (her mother has policed her since birth).

Why are you so tortured Maggie? Maggie is tortured by the nuns they hit her with rulers and her father spanked her too she still craves to be punished.

Why are you so tortured Maggie? Maggie is tortured by the video of the abortion she watched when she was in high school she just remembers something about vacuum-sucking like a vacuum cleaner sucking out all the little fetal bits.

The boys scrape away at her self-esteem, a psychic abortion.

Don't be such a pill Maggie they say.
Take your medicines like a good girl they say.
Shut up and take it they say.

Maggie has had trauma, yes she has. Most of this trauma Maggie has invited upon herself. Maggie has fucked and fucked until she was empty inside. Maggie has let so many men inside of her.

Maggie is all dried up now. It has all been vacuumed out. It has all been sucked away.

A hole, a hollow shell of who she used to be.

Maggie cantspeak. Maggie is a zombie. Maggie is bound and gagged and Maggie likes it.

The cat has got Maggie's tongue.

Maggie has only one more life to live.

Maggie sits and stares and considers the world. What does Maggie think of? Maggie wishes she was dead.

Maggie wants to lay down and stop instead of barreling forth blindly until she dies.

Maggie has RACING THOUGHTS. They follow each other one after each other no one loves her Marlon Brando doesn't love her Maggie is ugly Maggie is ugly and unloved Maggie should be dead Maggie is better off dead.

Maggie is a whore. Maggie is a whore.

Maggie doesn't want to actively die, she just wants to passively not live.

MALACHI

Malachi is burning up. The heat beats down on him. The sun is speaking to him. Tongues of fire. The sun is coming closer, closer. The sun—the source. Malachi can't hear what the sun has to say. The noises of the people blot out the sun's message. He is walking, walking, walking. He is walking on the gray concrete. No one looks at him. Blotted-out windows. Windows of the soul. No one dares look into his eyes. No one stops to help him. He watches a woman jogger feed her golden retriever a bottle of expensive water. She has devices in her ears which keep her from hearing. No one listens. Their air-conditioning mutes the helpless screams. A landscape of ringtones and mundanity. People talk to themselves. They talk, they talk to themselves but they don't say anything. Cell phone towers of Babble. They babble but they do not communicate. They walk down the streets talking to themselves, but Malachi is the one who is insane. Yes, Malachi is the one who is sick while people talk to their TV sets. Guillotined heads. The disembodied. Brainwashing of the lambs, the childlike. Yes they do not HEAR. Malachi's mission is to make them HEAR. They cannot HEAR. They do not want to HEAR the truth. They are deaf and dumb to the truth.

Malachi shields his hands from the bright light of his pure energy. Not his enemy. Who is his enemy? Who must be punished? The heat is making him confused. A flash: A shot in the arm.

He has been shot!
He's going down!

A sensation of immobility, a heaviness. He has been captured prisoner by the enemy. They had been following him, watching him everywhere on security cameras, in train stations. He began taking the bus. Still they found him. He is being forced under water, he can't breathe, he can't breathe, he is choking, choking on stale air . . . Yes he has known the silence, the stillness of death. He is not afraid. He is ready for his mission.

He waits for a sign, some sort of sign. Oh, yes, he remembers. He feels inside his pocket. His secret messages.

one life for the life of
thousands
&
a great fireball will erupt from the sky

The ink bleeds on his scripture. He places the two scraps of paper together. He puzzles over their meaning. Who is the one life? Is the instruction to kill or be killed? Thou Shalt Not Kill he mutters solemnly to himself. But, but, it says here: one life for the life of thousands. Is he being sent to kill the ministers of war? Or is he the flaming sacrifice on offering? Perhaps he has been sent here to be a martyr? A spiritual warrior? Perhaps he is the son? Perhaps he must die for their sins?

the son
the sun

The sun! He raises his head up again. The sun

blinds him. He is blinded. He sees planets, a planet of hope or a planet of demise?

THEY DO NOT HEAR
THEY MUST SEE

His mouth is moving. He is pronouncing utterances—are they coming from his mouth or from the sun?

They are all smote with blindness
the Lord has sent us to destroy it

So is that what he has been sent to do? Perhaps he must set fire to the sinful city? In order to shock them into waking. Wasn't Sodom and Gomorrah an act of terrorism, divined by God himself? An angel of vengeance, come to wreak havoc on the men who have raped and murdered the children the innocents yes who have raped and murdered the innocents. A pang, settled somewhere. His son! He turns towards his Father, the Light.

the son
the sun

No, he is called to a higher power. He must leave his home, his family. He is meant to communicate. But surely, not to kill? He turns his head upwards once more. The sun erases all meaning. Burning, burning up. He must burn up this city? He remembers the gasoline, the Book of Matches. But no, no, it says

one life for the life of
thousands

A REVELATION: the end of ends

he knows now what he was called to do.

MOMMY

Mommy stands up at her little island, her little island away from the world, her Formica island in the middle of her kitchen, and thoughtfully snaps iceberg lettuce into a bowl. She is thinking, thinking. Mommy is alone most of the time. Daddy is at work from 5 am until 7 pm (he drives two hours a day so that Mommy can live in her little house in the country). Mommy and Laci wait at the door at 7 pm for the garage door to open, for the beep of the security alarm. Mommy and Laci both run out to greet Daddy. A sign waits for him too, HOME SWEET HOME. And on the weekend Daddy spends the day at his home away from home Home Depot. Daddy likes to walk around smelling the manly things and running his hands over the wood used to build big sturdy things. Daddy is at work finishing the basement it needs to be finished nothing is ever finished in this house Daddy always has some project or another to occupy himself! He spends his weekends drilling and shaving away and Mommy calls him up for lunches of ham sandwiches and flavored iced tea! Or sometimes eggsalad sandwiches or turkey sandwiches! Daddy is always so appreciative Thank You Baby he says and always so complimentary This Is The Best Eggsalad I've Ever Had! Mommy twinkles under such praise. She knows how to keep a hubby happy! But Daddy is downstairs most of the time sometimes a thought creeps up—he is hiding from Mommy—but Mommy banishes the bad thought away. Yes it is Mommy and the TV and Laci. And Mommy's mommy is away in Florida visiting her gay son (Mommy's mommy may be a bit of a bigot, but the promise of poolside coladas and a deep tan to stain her wrinkly flesh irons out any ideological differences). Mommy is alone. Mommy and the TV. Mommy is watching one of those religious channels, it is an exorcism of housewives, the man smacks his hand on these women's foreheads and they fall down cured. Mommy wants to be cured of whatever dark thoughts she is thinking! That's why Mommy collects angels, the angels protect her from sad thoughts and bad thoughts and mad thoughts. She thinks about Maggie, her bad egg. She not-thinks about Maggie, her bad egg, instead she lovingly makes eggsalad for her hubby. (The key ingredient: lots and lots of mayonnaise!) Mommy doesn't count calories, Mommy counts smiles. Mommy keeps her recipes cards on little postcards with hearts on them, which she stores in a heart-shaped box. Mommy has so many hearts! Maggie her bad egg has a black black heart. When did Maggie go bad? Mommy wonders, not-wonders, her pudgy arm stirring, stirring the eggsalad, adding lots of mayo, as Daddy likes it (Mommy doesn't believe in diets). Mommy makes her eggsalad with LOVE. That is the real secret ingredient. And didn't Mommy make Maggie's lunches with love when she was growing up? Oh those wonderful, heartaching days. Mommy would cut Maggie's sandwiches into all sorts of fun shapes, like hearts, with her heart-shaped cookie-cutter. And she would make home-baked cookies for Maggie's lunch, and didn't she pack her everything she ever wanted? But Maggie wanted to leave the nest. But what is wrong with their beautiful nest? Maggie didn't want her heart shaped with a cookie-cutter, Maggie didn't care for their cookie-cutter lunches and cookie-cutter houses and cookie-cutter lives. Mommy's heart cries out for her Maggie. Not the Maggie that is now, Mommy doesn't know that Maggie, Mommy doesn't care to know that pale, unsmiling girl. Mommy's heart cries out for her baby girl, her baby bird with the mouth wide open for Mommy to drop food into her mouth. A salty tear drops into the eggsalad. A little salt won't hurt the flavor. Mommy is not crying for Maggie Mommy is crying tears of self-pity. She is an orphaned Mommy! The empty nest is such a tragedy, a tragedy. Other mommies she knows still see all of their children on the weekends, but Mommy only has one good child, the other is a bad, bad, girl, and will be sent to her room without any dinner. Mommy has kept Maggie's room just as it was. It has been decorated lovingly by Mommy—everything a girl could ever want! (although obviously Maggie wanted more). A flowery bedspread from Laura Ashley, porcelain statues of angels, a shelf of her china dolls Mommy and GrandMommy bought for her each year (one doesn't play with those dolls, one combs their hair lovingly and puts them away nicely). The dolls have not aged. The dolls still stare at Mommy when she goes to Maggie's room and dusts and has a nice cry. The roses on the Laura Ashley bedspread have faded. Mommy picks up each of the dolls lovingly. There is Snow White there is Scarlett O'Hara there is Sleeping Beauty. Mommy closes her eyes they flicker shut like the dolls and pictures her Maggie her Sleeping Beauty she wishes deep inside a wish so deep she cannot voice it that Maggie has simply pricked her finger and fallen asleep for these twenty years, and she will wake up and she will be her little girl again. And then Mommy wakes up and she is in Maggie's room like a time capsule, like a pink cave. Mommy wishes Maggie could go right back in her pink cave, and Mommy would keep Fetus Maggie warm and safe there and there would be no reason to push, push out into the great big scary world. Mommy wishes Maggie were still in utero. A thought flickers past Mommy's eggsalad stirring mind—if Maggie was a bad egg, should Mommy have gotten rid of her? NO NO NO Mommy suppresses that evil thought, she pushes it deep deep down like her roller flattening out the dough with which to make the bread with which to make Daddy's Stupendous Yummy Eggsalad Sandwich. She does think about Maggie, and whether Maggie would be evil and have an abortion. Secretly Mommy hopes promiscuous Maggie does get knocked up, because then she'll have no choice but to come home and live in her bedroom again, where she belongs, and Mommy will be the Mommy to Maggie and Maggie's baby. And the baby will be born out of wedlock, which is a sin, but a far lesser sin than murdering the baby. Because murdering babies is bad. Mommy doesn't think as she's stirring her eggsalad sandwich that the eggs she boiled and then smashed with her wooden spoon from Williams-Sonoma was actually an almost-baby, an almost-chicken baby, this is not something Mommy thinks about, it's unpleasant, and only people like Maggie bring up such unpleasant things that Mommy would rather not think about. Mommy is conflicted. Mommy is sad that Maggie doesn't call anymore, even though Mommy waits by the phone on Sundays like a hurt dog and then Daddy has to take her out for Brownie Sundaes at Chili's to cheer her up. But Mommy is in a way secretly glad that Maggie doesn't call anymore, because all Maggie does is bring up unpleasant things like war and drugs and the painfilled past, and Mommy feels like she wants to wash her brain out afterwards, because Maggie stirs up such unpleasant unnecessary things. And is this why? we're paying the big bucks to that expensive psych-ia-trist (Mommy can't pronounce it) so that he can turn our

Maggie against us? When are you coming home to visit? Mommy used to implore Maggie. She would cajole her, she would bribe her with nice pretty things to be purchased at the local mall! But Maggie has important things to do. Maggie can't be bothered. What could be more important than family? Mommy wonders. What could be more important than one's flesh-and-blood? We are the same flesh-and-blood Mommy implores Maggie, Maggie responds the same blood courses through all of us, and Mommy starts to tune out because either Maggie's being literal, which Mommy hates, or Maggie's giving her a lecture, or both. Mommy has an amazing ability to tune out. It's like when she's listening to the radio and she doesn't like what she hears and she changes the channel, changes the channel to the oldies station or the lite station on the FM dial where she can listen to pleasant nothings. That's what Mommy likes to listen to pleasant nothings. Or when Daddy whispers sweet nothings in her ear. Although Mommy doesn't like dirty talk she likes clean talk. Clean, sweet talk. Mommy likes to stay on the surface of life, she likes to stay on the small roads and not veer off into the highway. Life to Mommy is not a highway, Life is a small country road, it is a little bumpy for sure but it's safe and it's slow and it leads back home. Mommy should have locked Maggie up and never let her go. Mommy wishes Maggie was still on her training wheels. Mommy wishes she could walk around with Maggie on a leash like she does with Laci. Mommy wishes Maggie would bark and wag her tail joyfully when she sees Mommy like Laci does. Laci knows who her Mommy is. Laci loves her Mommy, yes she does, yes she does.

MAGGIE

There is so much suffering in the world Maggie knows but Maggie can only really feel her own pain.

Maggie is back on her meds. Maggie sends out an sos and only her psychiatrist calls her back so she decides to do what he says, since he cares.

Sometimes Maggie wakes up and her mind is full of potato chips and other times she is sure she is practically a genius.

Maggie has found God.

Maggie is God.

Perhaps, the psychiatrist says, we just need to change the prescriptions.

Maggie is MANIC. Maggie understands why Van Gogh cut off his ear. Maggie stays up all night washing dishes. She washes every dish, and then she washes the floor. On her hands and knees, on her hands and knees. Red impressions.

When Maggie was little Maggie wanted to marry God. She so desperately wanted to marry God. He was her first crush Maggie gets crushed by these men by the enormity of her desire for them.

Maggie remembers her knees kneeling on the pews her knees reddened Maggie is on her knees Maggie is on her knees Maggie wants to receive the holy wedding ring from God and they will live happily ever after.

Maggie wants to scream, to feel.

Maggie wishes to be a manicurist. Maggie thinks she would be a good manicurist. She could file other people's nails. Maggie needs a file to chisel away at the bars.

Maggie desires to be different. Maggie desires to be anything else than who she is.

Maggie thinks everything is an elaborate game to distract the living.

Maggie thinks she's going to suffocate in the woolen silence. She cannot breathe. She cannot breathe.

Perhaps, the psychiatrist says, we just need to tinker with the formula some more.

Maggie fucks just to feel alive. Just to feel real.

Question: How many bad boys does it take to screw Maggie?

Maggie is vertical but she would rather be horizontal.

Maggie is homeless now Maggie has no home she is sleeping on strangers' couches. She uses her overcoat as a blanket. It looks like a tent.

But at least Maggie is FREE. She is free from the MAN. She is free from the MACHINE.

She is not free from men in general, just the MAN.

Maggie needs to fuck the men who let her stay with them. She doesn't have to, but it is an implied contract.

She wakes up from their grimy beds, tousled and confused. She reaches for her pack of smokes. She cannot find her underwear. She doesn't remember the night before. The smell of tequila. A line of coke on the nightstand table.

Gone, gone, gone. Maggie is gone, gone, gone.

Whispers, whispers, about Maggie. Maggie who is diseased. Maggie who is distressed. SOS. Must not come too close to Maggie. Must not catch what Maggie's got.

Maggie has gone AWOL. The psychiatrist cannot reach Maggie, the psychiatrist cannot tinker with his mad experiment anymore.

In the forest predators would not come near Maggie, because Maggie is crazy, but here predators cum all over Maggie. Maggie is prey. Maggie gets down on her knees like she is praying.

Maggie has been living hand-to-mouth. Mouth-to-other-parts.

Maggie is stoned most of the time.

They throw stones, they throw stones.

Maggie is catatonic and drooling. She lets the men cum all over her. She lets them into all of her holes

the gutters

Maggie is cracked up. A good suburban girl like Maggie can't be smoking crack. Maggie is between a rock and a hard place.

Maggie went off her meds again but she can't think straight she is burning excess fuel.

It is all about brain chemicals now for Maggie. Maggie is her own chemistry experiment.

Pretty, pretty, pills. Maggie is not so pretty anymore. She is bloated and tired. Maggie looks like an old woman.

Maggie cannot sell her body. She can sell her

body only on the discount rack. The rack-and-the-screw.

One should only screw Maggie in the dark. She's not pretty to look at.

Maggie needs her nightlight on.

It is the disease raging in Maggie. It is the disease.

WARNING SIGNS. WHAT TO WATCH FOR.

Perhaps, the psychiatrist says to Mommy and Daddy, we need to bring her in for closer observation.

If we can find Maggie
Where in the world is Maggie?

Maggie is a sick monkey.

Maggie refuses to be a lemming. She will fall off a cliff if that means not being a lemming.

It is the Fourth of July weekend. It is hot and she is staying in a dark place. Maggie is in a dark place with no A/C. Maggie is in HELL.

Do you have a plan now, Maggie?

Maggie has been storing up her pills like a Maggie-squirrel.

Maggie doesn't want to actively die but she doesn't want to passively keep on living.

Maggie is tired. Maggie is so tired. Maggie just wants to go sleepy-sleep-sleep, yes, good night, angel, yes, good night.

Maggie just wants to sleep. Maggie is Sleeping Beauty.
She wants to sleep forever and ever.

It is the Fourth of July weekend and Maggie wants to be FREE.
Her Dependence Day

The fireworks
A ticking-time-bomb
Tick, tock, tick, tock, thermometer

She scrawls on a piece of paper: Goodbye world. Goodbye, Mommy. Goodbye, Daddy. I am so sorry for being such a bad, bad girl. I am so sorry for the trouble I have caused. It was nobody's fault. I just can't bear the pain anymore. It's all so hard.

Maggie signs the piece of paper "Your Maggie" and then a smiley face. ☺

Maggie signs her suicide note with a smiley face ☺

Maggie takes a bottle of Smirnoff into the bathtub and her collection of smiley pills and sleep-sleep pills.

Maggie takes her clothes off.
Maggie is naked as the day she was born. Except a lot bigger.
Maggie locks the door.
Maggie waits for the whoosh and the end. She waits for the darkness to come. She waits for the void.

Maggie rushes towards the light mute yet violent

Maggie sends out invisible sos's

The roar of sirens
The men bang down the door
The men in their white, white coats
The pharmacists
The butchers

A body on a slab. A sacrificial victim.

Her exhausted and brutalized body

Maggie is worn out. Maggie has stopped working.

Do you know your name?
Say something, say something damn it!

With a great big slap she was brought into this
world screaming without saying a word . . .

MALACHI

He is looking down below at the RUSH HOUR, the swarm of crawling black bugs with shiny shells, self-righteous shells of security. He wears a sign around his neck: THOU SHALT NOT KILL. He speaks in scripture. He uses their words against them. Still they pretend the truths he utters are mad. They will not listen, they will only SEE. A bolt of lightning. A bolt of truth. He will be the sacrificial lamb. They who are led to slaughter.

The sacrificial lamb roasted on a fire. A pit of flames. Down below.

He shields his eyes to wait for directions. The city is all a-blaze. They are at war. Whistles and booms drown out the chatterings of everyday. God has rained down fiery vengeance upon this concrete city.

It is his sign.

One life for the life of
thousands

One must not look back. One cannot look back, or else be consumed by the flames.

THEY MUST SEE. THEY MUST SEE A SPECTACLE OF HUMAN SUFFERING.

The gasoline can stolen from the station. He is no ordinary thief. He is on a mission from God. The Book of Matches. The Book. Burning, burning.

And then—the scream. The distorted groans of an impassioned martyr. Hurled headlong flaming from the sky.

there fell a great star from heaven, burning as if it were a lamp

MOMMY

Yes Maggie is in trouble Mommy and Daddy are coming to get her they are barreling forth blindly on the highway, on the highway of life, they have come to scoop Maggie up from the floor what is left of her and deposit her in her pretty pink bedroom back home. The psychiatrist has called. Maggie has been rushed to the hospital. Mommy and Daddy rush to save her. They rush to claim her. They have come to recover their daughter. Will she have a pricetag dangling from her toes? The hot hell or the icy morgue. Stored in the meat cooler like the other Jane Does. Maggie should have been a Jane Does-Not. How could this have happened to a girl from such a good background? From such a nice family? Mommy and Daddy are hurtling along the highway, they have come to recover their child, they have come to recover her childhood before it is too late! Or if it is too late they must collect their wilted consolation prize and bury her properly, in a nice dress with roses, yes, and roses for the ceremony, yes, that would be lovely, and we will ask Father Sullivan, yes. They are hurtling along Daddy is driving too fast Daddy you're driving too fast you're scaring me and Mommy is worrying, worrying herself sick. They are hurtling along. And then—STOP. Daddy must hit the brakes and Mommy almost hits her dear little redface on the dashboard. Must be some sort of trafficjam says Daddy and Mommy oh dears oh dears her daughter is in the hospital with a drip-drip and she must get there to take care of her! and bathe her and clothe her and bring her home 4-ever and ever! But oh why did Maggie try to hurt herself it must be true she must be a sick sick girl she must really be bipolar-manic-depressive-schizophrenic or whatever, Mommy and Daddy can't think of any of that no no not in this family, no no of course not, we put our trust in the Lord of course, he is our Light and our Savior, Maggie just needs to see the Light! So she will look away from the Light! And doesn't Maggie know that it's a Sin! To look towards the Light when it's not one's time to go! And a girl must always go gracefully! And Mommy wonders what these doctors are telling Maggie in the hospital, are they telling her it's all her mother's fault, that's nonsense of course it's Maggie's brain chemicals of course! They got a bad one that's right they got a devil when they had ordered an angel and they would like to return it! Although of course no Maggie's not up yet Daddy reminds her oh yes of course Mommy remembers Maggie has not woken up yet but as soon as Mommy gets there she is sure Maggie will perk right up! They have come to a full STOP and Daddy gets out of his car to see what is making all the ruckus it's Fourth of July weekend of course but they are at a full stop! When they have places to go things to do! Mommy has to sit vigil over her Maggie! This time Maggie won't sass her back because she'll be sleeping! Her little Sleeping Beauty! And she'll bathe and brush her little girl! Daddy comes back and Daddy is grim he is serious so serious. Mommy's heart leaps. Her man. Some maniac he says. Some maniac has jumped off the bridge. Oh dear oh dear says Mommy. Mommy's heart is all a-flutter. Her heart isn't so good lately you know. What with the Maggie and now this. She just can't take any more news. Mommy can't imagine what would make a person do such a thing. Such a pointless act. It is all so pointless so pointless Mommy says. Daddy agrees. Mommy finds it all deeply unpleasant. Mommy thinks of the man she thinks of the man's poor mother probably worried sick it's almost as if Maggie did this just to hurt her yes she did didn't she what a bad bad child a bad apple she is yes she is that Maggie perhaps there are just bad apples in the world Mommy thinks and then she tells herself what she has been saying the whole trip into the big bad wolf of a city, into its cave with the glistening fangs, that she's not to blame, that no one's to blame, that some people are just bad apples yes bad seeds and after all when things like this happen maybe some people just have the Devil inside of them after all remember remember it was nobody's fault yes it was nobody's fault it was nobody's fault.

ACKNOWLEDGMENTS

If it wasn't for Lidia Yuknavitch and her Chiasmus Press, I doubt *O Fallen Angel* would or could have been published, and it is to this writer, and this press, and to all the tiny presses still publishing wild and high-risk literature today, that this reissue is dedicated. And that earlier moment for me—so conclusive—reading Lidia's then-story "Loving Dora" in an issue of *Another Chicago Magazine (ACM)* immediately after it was published, which my boyfriend, now longtime partner, helped edit at the time— the sick rush of language, the witty explosion of the Freudian myth, even the obsession with

Francis Bacon! It took me a few years to get up my nerve to try to write my own novels, and knowing virtually nothing about publishing then (how I wish I was still so naïve), when I saw somewhere (a list in *Poets & Writers?*) that this writer Lidia Yuknavitch had a press, and was having a contest for books that were "Undoing the Novel," I thought I'd send her my books, if anyone would get them, she would. I felt sure of it. How speechless her foreword makes me— how intensely literature moves her, calling to mind our mentor (for her, in real life, for me, only spiritually) Kathy Acker writing in *Great Expectations* that "a narrative is an emotional moving." I really want to acknowledge the writers that believed in the book before its publication—Lily Hoang, who selected *OFA* in the contest, Chris Kraus, Vanessa Place, and Karen Finley, who provided early blurbs. And the other writers who I met or began corresponding with around the time the book came out that I felt such a kinship with and were supportive in crucial ways—Pamela Lu, Kate Durbin, Suzanne Scanlon, Danielle Dutton, Amina Cain, Bhanu Kapil, Gina Abelkop, Jackie Wang, Masha Tupitsyn, Jen Karmin, Anne Marie Rooney, Megan Milks, Rachel Levitsky, Rebecca Loudon, Mattilda Bernstein Sycamore, Blake Butler,

Laurie Weeks, the poets and writers behind presses like Nightboat Books, Action Books, Les Figues, and Belladonna. And to the supportive radicals within the Chiasmus community—Lance Olsen, Gina Frangello, Trevor Dodge, and Steve Tomasula especially. Thanks to the very few who wrote perceptively about this vicious little novella at the time, and I think really got the project—Blake at *HTML Giant*, Anne Yoder at *The Millions*, Dennis Cooper at his blog, *DC's*, Michael Schaub at *Bookslut* especially. And other writers and visionaries now, added to the crucial list above, who I met later, who I write in communication with—Sofia Samatar, Grant Maierhofer, Douglas Martin, Gregory Howard, Matias Viegener, T. Clutch Fleischmann, Adrian Nathan West, Sheila Heti, Azareen Van Der Vliet Oloomi, Stephanie LaCava. To the excellent novelists Heidi Julavits and Brian Morton, who continue to employ me to teach writing, which allows me to write weird texts that are never driven by the market. Thinking about this first book, and how incredibly difficult in a way it was for me to get my early work published, I want to think about the editors and readers who believed in my work, even when I was a nobody (I'm still hopefully a nobody, thank god), even when my work was formally inventive or antagonistic or overly intellectual, completely changed from text to text, extremely angry or emotional, and often the polar opposite of "commercial" or "reader-friendly" or whatever—Lidia Y., Chris and Hedi El Kholti at Semiotext(e), Amy Scholder, Sarah McCarry at Guillotine, Cal Morgan, and now the wonderfully perceptive Sofia Groopman at Harper Perennial—what on earth made you agree to reissue this! Thank you. To the indefatigable, seriously, Mel Flashman, who has championed my little books to be reissued over the past couple of years. Ali Shamas Qadeer, you are a wonderful designer/godsend/reader; thanks so much for the cover design of this book. As before, I want to acknowledge Malachi Ritscher, whose act of public immolation as protest against the Iraq war partially catalyzed this work, even though you are not my street preacher Malachi. As always, I want to thank my partner in crime/ constant collaborator, John Vincler—fellow Catholic Midwestern exile for whom art is a way of protest and life, who always laughed when I read out loud from these pages or was consistently the face of amusement in the back of the room at my severe reading from it, when no one else in the room knew how to react at all (when there were really any people in the room!), and has always encouraged me to do more in the work, and, more than anyone, has allowed me to move into new rooms with my work, to die and be reborn with every new text—how we stood in my little office in the Pilsen neighborhood of Chicago and laughed and laughed and danced with delight when we got the e-mail now 8 or 9 years ago that, finally, I was going to be published, this book! How you've always urged me on, how I love you.

ABOUT THE AUTHOR

Kate Zambreno is also the author of *Green Girl* and *Heroines*. She is at work on a series of books about time, memory, and the persistence of art. *Book of Mutter* is forthcoming from Semiotext(e) in March 2017. *Drifts* is forthcoming from Harper Perennial in early 2018.

P.S.

About the author

About the book

Insights,
Interviews
& More . . .

Read on

Interview with Kate Zambreno

by Anne K. Yoder

ZAMBRENO'S FIRST NOVEL *O Fallen Angel* reads like the bastard offspring of an orgy between John Waters's *Polyester*, Elfriede Jelinek's *Lust*, and Oliver Stone's *Natural Born Killers*. Lily Hoang said of the book, "*O Fallen Angel* examines the suburban family with ruthless elegance. Here is a novel, done and undone, a brazen mirror reflecting the twenty-first century."

AY: I'd like to hear more about the inspiration for your novel, *O Fallen Angel*, and specifically the inspiration you derived from Francis Bacon's *Three Studies for Figures at the Base of a Crucifixion*, which he based on a scene from *The Oresteia*. Of his painting, Bacon said, "I tried to create an image of the effect it [*The Oresteia*] produced inside me." One connection that came to mind is that it seems you attempt to recreate the effect that mainstream suburban, Midwestern culture produces within you. Reading the novel with Bacon in mind made me think of his screaming popes via the religious oppression, the psychiatric disturbances, and the authorial vitriol and scorn doled throughout. Were they somewhere in the back of your mind while writing too?

KZ: With Bacon, yes, I was trying to channel the effect that his paintings produced within me... I am really interested in what Deleuze has to say about Bacon's figures, how Bacon is painting these chaotic nervous systems, and in a way with a book like *OFA* I thought of myself as a portraitist I guess, but with language, exorcising both Bacon's triptych as well as the portraits of Marlene Dumas, and trying in a way to paint not characters but nervous systems, flayed and flawed and committing desperate acts of self-immolation. I lived for a bit in London and I became obsessed with the Bacon room at the Tate Britain, his orange paintings especially filled me with such a delirious violence, and I think I am always trying to write to them, write to his diseased mouths and paralyzed figures. The scream in general fascinates me, those who have had their language stolen from them, how to reproduce that on the page—Munch's *Scream* and Helene Weigel's grotesque mouth wide open in *Mother Courage*—and especially with this project I was interested in writing these figures (I keep on calling them figures! but that's what they are to me, or grotesques, grotesques I care for, not characters) that are completely inarticulate or stricken with a sort of wordless riot, as my Maggie character is, my modern hysterical Dora-daughter, or my Malachi prophet, my homeless Septimus Smith from *Mrs. Dalloway*, and yes Mommy too. Mommy is deeply, deeply unhappy but she lacks any way to articulate this, to express any individual expression, she is a member of Kant's minority, who just wants to be a cutesy cow grazing on Snax Mix. ►

Interview with Kate Zambreno (*continued*)

Through all this I am channeling my own feelings of impotence, of alienation, of desperation, the feeling sometimes that most are mute and deaf and dumb to all of the horrors of existence, preferring to exist in their banal languages and worlds, in many ways in terms of an exercise in language I was trying to write to the banality of clichés, how they mold our minds, and of the banality of the exclamation point, the emoticon. Everyone who reads it gets that this is a novel set in Midwestia, in suburbia, and it is, sure, that's where the impulse began, my environment, but it's just as much to me a novel about liberals in cities who easily accept the status quo and would rather discuss *American Idol* or some shit than gay rights or rights for women or the environment and really really about a country at war and pretending not to be at war. It's an extremely political novel, a novel screeching against the war and the banality of evil. A friend said to me: Mommy is the Bush administration. And yes! Yes that's true. I really loved that. But it's not just the Bush administration. It's not just the convenient enemies I was trying to write to in this book, and failing, and I will always try to write to, again and again.

Not just the red states and Midwestia but the society at large.

And it's great you bring up *The Oresteia* because besides *Mrs. Dalloway* it's the other text

I'm trying to rewrite in *O Fallen Angel*, not just Bacon purging the Furies and the scream of Clytaemestra and Cassandra in many of his triptychs, but also that, in many ways I frame the book like a Greek tragedy, with choruses, and I will always try to rewrite *The Oresteia* in any work of this type, in all of my political work. And I love Bacon's screaming popes, all of his patriarch paintings, his blue businessmen. I think Mommy is the real patriarch in this novel, so she's not a screaming pope, she uses manipulation and sweet expressions and not brute force, along with the furniture and her statues she will try to rearrange her children's minds.

AY: To a review in *The Rumpus* that criticized your lack of empathy for your characters, you responded: "If anything it's a novel about ALIENATION, and I am in many ways alienating my readers, drawing from theater, Brecht's A-effect, Artaud's notion of the plague, Karen Finley. But I think it's a disappointing conventional read to expect all novels to be about characters, a novel in which character and relationships are privileged, and I think of that as a sort of MFA-itis." I understand this to mean that you believe MFA programs are overly influential, and at their worst, a homogenizing force in the way they shape their students' narrative expectations. Javier Marías once said that if he were ever to start a writing school, translation would be its touchstone. What would a writing program designed by Kate Zambreno look like? ▶

Interview with Kate Zambreno *(continued)*

KZ: Yes, I think MFA programs can be homogenizing forces and churn out literature that is hygenic and functional. But of course not all MFA programs are like this. I think my main problem is how many MFA programs for fiction are structured, and who is hired in most of these programs, who does the hiring, and how hybridity or dancing along genres is really discouraged in many programs, in my totally limited observation because I neither have an MFA nor did I study creative writing as an undergraduate. But it seems the focus of most creative writing fiction programs is still realism, still a traditional focus on character and plot, and a focus on the story that is about the human heart (an idea I'm stealing from the writer Steve Tomasula). So I think at least in fiction programs works that are engaging with philosophy or with theory or are queer or feminist or radical or about the body and trauma and abjectness or are totally weirdo-schizo-whatever, you know, fucking with form, trying to invent new forms, any textual transgressions, any beautiful little monsters, are probably shredded in workshop.

A review of *O Fallen Angel* said that if the novel had been workshopped, that the teacher would freak out, basically. And I think it would have been savaged in most MFA fiction programs and any rawness or rough edges or anything instinctual about it would be sort of smoothed away to attempt to reach approval by committee, both in the workshop and then in some sort of thesis situation. So I think in my writing program I would really try to steer away from the notion of a piece "working" or "functioning" because a text is not supposed to work, lawnmowers are supposed to work and cut grass, a text is supposed to make you explode, agitated, or at least feel something, feel and then think, think and then feel, act, not just pat the pretty language or sigh and feel a little wistful or a little good about yourself or whatever. So I would want my writing program to be a radical laboratory; it would be about changing society through the text.

As Camus has said, if you want to be a philosopher, write novels. Some of the most exciting urgent public intellectuals and philosophers are creative writers. In my totally hypothetical writing program I would encourage students to be completely promiscuous in their reading, to read philosophy and theory and become obsessed with art and film, to become obsessed with something outside of their craft, like I don't know, a different religion or anything outside of themselves, but then to burrow deep inside of themselves too, to learn new languages and read anything but the obvious books, then maybe read the obvious ones again, read in translation, engage with the world and have experiences. Fuck up a lot. Write about it. Go on weird travels. Always bring books with you. Write about the travels and the books that you're carrying with you. And as opposed to the workshop process there will be ▶

Interview with Kate Zambreno *(continued)*

readings and mentor relationships set up and
others will rigorously engage with your work
but never offer prescriptions, only guidance.
A program that is what Woolf has called a
writing apprenticeship, to learn how to inhabit
the necessary private space of a writer, to be a
writer, not just how to get a story published in
X, Y, or Z publication. But I would also want
activism to be a prominent feature. Not that I
consider myself any authority to head such a
writing program. I would want to be in such a
program. There will be no teachers! Everyone
will be students! No degrees! No diplomas!
Just writing books and learning how to be a
citizen of the world.

AY: You reviewed your novel, *O Fallen Angel*,
for the blog *We Who Are About to Die*. It's an
insightful and entertaining introduction to
the book. In it you claim: "My characters
don't touch each other, but they want to
connect and they're all suffocating in their
cells. It is a stupid, terrible book, about the
stupid and the terrible." While this statement
is simultaneously ironic and earnest, self-
conscious and comic (if all four qualities can
coexist at once), it demands the question, why
write a stupid and terrible book about the
stupid and the terrible?

KZ: Well, for the first statement, the book
being stupid and terrible, I think in many

ways for this project I was interested in really bad writing, I guess this is how I'm influenced by Acker, in clichés, in the smiley face Maggie uses to sign her suicide note, there's a line ending a Maggie section "The first cut is the deepest," which I'm totally quoting from that Cat Stevens song, tunneling inside Maggie's head, and at this moment of total self-annihilation over an ex-lover Maggie is really trying to be deep and poetic but she's just a photocopy, a profound but then ultimately banal photocopy of a pop song, and I'm interested in all that, how our brains are colonized with well-tread language, yet we're convinced we're terribly profound and individual. When I read that line at readings people always are kind of silent, but I find it so funny—like look! look how bad and awful this is! this is really bad writing! but people are silent because I think they're a bit embarrassed for me, which I love. And look how mean I'm being, how cruel! It's a terrible, terrible book!

My view of humanity at least in this novel is cruel and caricatured; I am playing with these grotesques, and when you think of Bakhtin on Rabelais and the grotesque, the grotesque is cruel and mean and just completely destructive humor. I am more interested in this book and my political writing in general at this moment in the destruction, the total annihilation, as opposed to finding a sort of corrective or moment ofoptimism. So it's a terrible book, it's about terrible things, and it says terrible things. ▶

But besides this authorial act of spraying acid, the family I write about in the book are grotesques, they are caricatures, and they seem innocent and normal and average, but I am saying that amidst all of this banality there's something really dangerous in terms of how we swallow horrible things happening because they make us uncomfortable and ignore all the fucked-up-ness and like let's talk about *The Bachelor* as opposed to Haiti and as a society we're still totally, totally repressed, as represented in this book by the Mommy character. Everything's airbrushed but underneath everything's shit. It's one view of the world, it's not the only one, it's certainly a pretty dystopic and scathing one.

I'm circling back to that *Rumpus* reviewer's critiquing me for not being empathetic—I think being political is being empathetic, by calling attention to who is actually silenced and oppressed, and how the family functions as the oppressor as well as other oedipal structures, other mommies and daddies, government, religion, etc. But it's funny the idea that I'm not empathetic to the people doing the normalizing and oppressing and silencing. Fuck it. I'm not. When the British modernist Anna Kavan started writing her tripped-out dystopic works after, you know, being institutionalized and then living through the bombings in England and seeing the effects of war, she said to her publisher, Peter Owen, "That's just how I see the world now." And I always think about that.

Reprinted with permission. A longer version of this August 2010 interview first appeared in The Millions, *where Anne K. Yoder is a staff writer. Her work has appeared in* Fence, Bomb, *and* Tin House *among other publications. She is a member of Meekling Press, a collective micropress based in Chicago. Currently she is working on a novel,* The Enhancers, *about coming of age in a pharmaceutically driven society.* ∾

Review of *O Fallen Angel*

by Michael Schaub

WHAT DO YOU SAY about an American gospel
that beats the shit out of you?

It's come up before, of course, though it's
been a while. Gone is William S. Burroughs,
gone is Hubert Selby Jr., gone is Kathy Acker.
Now we have Bret Easton Ellis, who's as original
as a porn DVD and as punk rock as a Walmart.
We have shock, but never for a reason. I have to
mention Acker again; it's almost sacrilegious to
think of anyone being like her, but some of those
who loved her have been hoping, secretly, for an
heiress or heir. So enter Kate Zambreno, who is
as much Acker as she is Woolf, as much Angela
Carter as she is Elfriede Jelinek. (These are the
four names most closely associated with
Zambreno, and with good reason—it's almost
impossible to read *O Fallen Angel*, her brilliant
2010 novel, without thinking of Zambreno
as a perfected synthesis, but a wholly original
one, of all four of those authors.)

I'll try not to make too much of the fact that
I wrote, accidentally, "holy" for "wholly" in that
last sentence. But you can't get around it—*O
Fallen Angel* is a gospel and a fairy tale, and it is
uniquely American. If I were religious, I'd be
tempted to call Zambreno a prophet. I'm not,
but I'm tempted to anyway. Countless writers
have attempted what Zambreno does here—a
beautiful, unique, angry-as-fuck satire about

contemporary America, wrapped up in a wrenching family psychodrama. But in the last decade, the attempts were either too subtle or too dumb. There is no subtlety in this book; there is a good deal of enraged fuck-you bravado, cut with almost unbearable sadness and desolation. And every note of it is perfect.

There are three people here, or three kind-of people, the jury's out on at least one of them, maybe more. Mommy is a midwestern housewife—she's fat, with a fat husband, a son who's probably going to be fat once his own kid grows up. The family eats too much. They buy too much. They are xenophobic and racist and homophobic. They think of themselves as happy. They are not.

Maggie is her daughter, her estranged daughter, living in the big city. She is bipolar, drug-addicted, suicidal. She is a fairy tale heroine. Or as Mommy would say, with her breathless exclamations, She is a fairy tale heroine! She is a good girl! Maggie:

> *always lets them get at least to third base which is finger-fucking*

> *usually she lets them get to home plate*

> *And Sleeping Beauty was slipped a mickey and raped. Or she just let him inside of her because he was pleading and insistent and she wanted him to call her again.*

> *And Sleeping Beauty wanted to be liked and had terribly low self-esteem so when* ▶

he said that she was the prettiest girl in all the land she gave him a blow-job, even though her jaw locks sometimes.

And Sleeping Beauty pretended to be asleep but really she died inside and then she let Prince Charming cum between her tits and in her hair as he breathed Yeah Bitch Take It.

And Sleeping Beauty didn't make him wear a condom and now she has pelvic inflammatory disease and crotch-itch and genital warts, but oh, the memories.

And then there's Malachi, about whom it's hard to say anything. He is a fallen angel and a confused prophet; he could well be the author here, he could stand for her. He is named after, one supposes, Malachi Ritscher, who four years ago burned himself to death in Chicago, protesting the Iraq War.

So, three voices: denial (Mommy), despair (Maggie), and something unnameable that somehow combines the two and their opposites (Malachi). It is not an easy book to explain. It is a very easy book to feel. Mommy disowns Maggie; Maggie disowns life; Malachi disowns the world. It's a lot like listening to three operas at once, all dissonant and frenetic and sad, and not being able to turn any of them off. *O Fallen Angel* is the angriest book I've read in years, possibly since Stephen Wright's *Going Native,* which shares nothing with this novel stylistically, but feels like the same plaintive, enraged, confused scream.

And like all anger, it's impossible to synthesize or summarize; it loses everything in translation. I've spent months thinking about it nearly every day, and I've largely given up on trying to explain it. It's how you feel at your worst moments; it's less a book than a Molotov cocktail of a story. It will make you think of Acker, sure, but it's a different angel with a different harp. It's something only Kate Zambreno could have done, and it's brave and scared and indispensable.

Michael Schaub is a writer, book critic, and regular contributor to NPR Books. *His work has appeared in the* Washington Post, San Francisco Chronicle, Portland Mercury, *and* Austin Chronicle, *among other publications. A native of Texas, he now lives in Portland, Oregon. This review first appeared on* Bookslut *in August 2010. Reprinted with permission.* ∼

Postcard from America

by Kate Zambreno

I HAVE JUST RETURNED from a lengthy road trip
through the Midwest back to Brooklyn, New
York, where for the time being I live. We drove
for three days to a log cabin that my Italian-
American grandfather helped build almost a
century ago, way up in the Upper Peninsula of
Michigan, a half hour drive away from the
nearest incorporated town. (He got a share of
the cabin in exchange for legal work before he
quit the law to be a butcher.) For days on end I
held our terrier Genet on a pillow on my lap, as
he agitated at bridges and rumble strips. It was
hot as hell, in the midst of this dreary "heat
dome," in which the center and Eastern parts of
our country are immersed right now. My body
was perennially in burning discomfort while
trapped in our small Honda, as that week I just
entered the third trimester of pregnancy, and we
had to stop every two hours for me to stretch,
empty my bladder, get the weight of the dog off
me. I was downing so much water to stop the
contractions I was having from the heat, that
strange tightening feeling, like my stomach was
going to explode. I have never been so sick in my
life of public bathrooms—of wiping down seats,
of the cheap toilet paper that gets stuck in your
pubic hair, of waddling my uncomfortable
strange body through doors, the same fast food
chains, everything almost identical. What
slightly disturbed me this trip was the amused
or adoring or concerned gaze I received from so

many strangers—who saw me as a very pregnant and sweaty woman in a short cotton dress with her little black dog, who saw me as very much a woman, an impending mother, something both visible and totally unthreatening, not the usual suspicious looks we sometimes got as city people in small Midwestern towns. I didn't like it. But as we drove through the various highways and roads, through Pennsylvania, through Ohio, through Michigan, I was especially disturbed, rattled, by the looming highway signs VOTE FOR TRUMP! MAKE A AMERICA GREAT AGAIN! Or the HILLARY FOR PRISON signs. Or just the singular, fucking scary, almost onomatopoeic TRUMP. I didn't see that many—but the ones I did see looked like ominous humid beacons that I couldn't quite believe. Trump is everywhere—it is now three months away from the election, the same week my daughter is expected to be born—we were finally a bit separated from the news in the woods, when before we were trapped in that endless cycle of constant refresh, horror, distraction, but every time we looked at the *Times* I joked to my partner it felt like the *Trump Times*, it was all they were covering, his every racist belch and shocking pronouncement. I just logged on to double-check and the Olympics is front page—that jingoistic distraction, yet I watch the clips on YouTube too, in awe at the American female gymnastic team, needing some sort of what Lauren Berlant might call a national feeling, or national sentimentality— and then every other fucking article is about ▶

Postcard from America *(continued)*

Trump, Trump's dad, Trump being down in the polls, what darned thing did Trump say today, the Trump kids. This summer—this summer has been so terrible, seemingly apocalyptic, there is a darkness to the landscape, to reference David Wojnarowicz. Every day we get news of the regular and horrific police brutality against black Americans, the surveillance and murder of black Americans that had gone undocumented for so many years, every day this summer there seems to be another report of a massacre or bombing in the world, the massacre at the Orlando nightclub, where LGBT and Latinx Americans were specifically targeted, the attacks during a Bastille Day celebration in Nice, France, in an airport in Turkey, in a hospital in Pakistan, some claimed by the Islamic state, others the result of individual attacks of toxic masculinity, but all simplified and politicized when coming out of the brutal and banal mouths of corrupt politicians, paid for by banks and the NRA, a xenophobia that is further radicalizing alienated Muslim kids who are consistently told they're not American, or that America hates them, this erosion of the gray zone that is ISIS's main intent, which the Trump fire-breathing mouth-machine just feeds into. Almost every week I hear about some mass shooting in this country, where unhinged men and boys born on paranoia and fear get access to assault rifles, and nothing happens. There were just two women raped and strangled and murdered while out running in the fucking broad daylight, in Boston and Queens. There are laws being passed in states like North Carolina criminalizing transgendered people from using the bathroom of their chosen gender, while trans and gay youths are still the most vulnerable to not only depression and suicide, but rape and murder. Trump's VP pick is the monster governor from Indiana who tried to put a bill into place demanding that fetuses need burials, and all the time all over this country the rights of women to receive accessible and safe abortions are being peeled away, even Clinton's VP pick is against helping poor women, predominantly women of color, from having access to safe and legal abortions, because they cannot afford it. This is not my grief, I do not own it, I cannot appropriate it, but it is my grief as an American, and I'm reminded of that line in David Wojnarowicz's jeremiad, *Close to the Knives*, lines that I could tattoo on my ever expanding and discontented body, I've quoted them so often: "I want to throw up because we're supposed to quietly and politely make house in this killing machine called America and pay taxes to support our own slow murder and I'm amazed we're not running amok in the streets, and that we can still be capable of gestures of loving after lifetimes of all this." He is writing amidst the Culture Wars and the NEA Four and Jesse Helms, amidst the death of his friends and fellow artists from AIDS, ▶

his beloved Peter Hujar, the disintegration of his own body also dying of the disease providing more urgency to the pages, the erasure of the crisis of AIDS and gay citizens from the national narrative, he is writing, no, not amidst, but against, and the entire series of essays is a scream against a wasteland of a country and a wasting body, and with that hatred, that vitriolic anger, some sort of love amidst the pessimism, some sort of radiant despair in his work, the videos, the photographs, the writing, in these acts of protest. I didn't come to writing with any sense of decorum or craft, with ideas of character or plot or narrative, with the stuff brained inside creative writing workshops or MFA programs, or even literature classes, I didn't even know when I started writing, if what I was writing were essays or novels or poetry or plays or what was it, knew nothing of publishing market mandates about what the reader wants, I came to writing as an amateur yet obsessive student of avant-garde performance and theater, of Brecht's A-effect, of Artaud's theater of cruelty, of Karen Finley as a daughter of Artaud with her raging monologues of victims and victimizers, of Sarah Kane's mournful and grotesque violence, like from the ancient Greeks. The art that really spoke to me was that of an excessive elegy, was tacky and angry, like David W's video "A Fire in my Belly," the St. Sebastian imagery, the ants crawling on the Crucifix. I'm realizing now that it's David Wojnarowicz's rage against provincial minds and Catholicism that I relate to the most, like Thomas Bernhard and Elfriede Jelinek's acidic novels against the ghosts of Austria's past, the banality of evil represented so often in the oppressive family structure. Around the time I began writing *O Fallen Angel*—around the summer of 2007, I think—I was binge-reading the novels of Elfriede Jelinek, really studying them, and wondering for me what an American political novel, post-Acker, would look like that was agitprop, that utilized a banal and complacent language as a sort of weaponry. (It made me so happy when I read the letters of Kathy Acker and Ken Wark just published by Semiotext(e), to realize that Kathy Acker was seriously reading Elfriede Jelinek in translation.) I was stalled from various larger projects and *O Fallen Angel* really began as a stylistic experiment, I had finished Jelinek's *Women as Lovers* and liked the sing-songy diptych structure, the way she could house larger social critiques within a text of the family, I thought, what would this look like if it was a sort of Midwestern Gothic? That was what I felt fated to write, novels of Midwest claustrophobia and rage, a triptych like Francis Bacon's paintings, a cruel, almost caricatured tale of the psychosis of the American family during wartime. I was so fucking angry and politically depressed that summer, as angry as I think I'm feeling scared and politically depressed this summer, ▶

Postcard from America (*continued*)

angry at the Bush administration and the Iraq war and conventions of gender and identity that I felt suffocated into, I felt impotent, and I felt angry, I had been thinking a lot about this man in Chicago who had just set himself on fire off the highway in protest against the war, and thinking of this girl I used to be very close with, from a South Side Irish Catholic family, who had committed suicide only a couple years earlier, and thinking of a comfortable racism and sexism and homophobia and xenophobia amidst a certain kind of white bourgeois family, and I was living in a Pilsen high-rise walk-up without air-conditioning in the worst July, feeling sweaty and angry and in some sort of state of an ecstatic trance, and this work came off fast—in under two months—like a protest, a scream, a song in my head. It feels so far away from my concerns now as a writer—I am more interested in my recent work, perhaps, now in a melancholy sort of elegy, than in vitriolic satire, but I am still interested in the link between these two, how to write of a historical memory, of ghosts, how both contain mourning. I admire *OFA's* energy, its intensity, its incredibly bad taste—sometimes, I wonder, if the past eight years have made me complacent. ❧

KZ
Brooklyn, NY
8/12/2016